BONE'S GOLD

by

KEN FARMER

Cover by: K.R. Farmer

AUTHOR

 Ken Farmer didn't write his first full novel until he was sixty-nine years of age. He often wonders what the hell took him so long. At age seventy-seven...he's currently working on novel number twenty-five.

Ken spent thirty years raising cattle and quarter horses in Texas and forty-five years as a professional actor (after a stint in the Marine Corps). Those years gave him a background for storytelling...or as he has been known to say, "I've always been a bit of a bull---t artist, so writing novels kind of came naturally once it occurred to me I could put my stories down on paper."

Ken's writing style has been likened to a combination of Louis L'Amour and Terry C. Johnston with an occasional Hitchcockian twist...now that's a combination.

In addition to his love for writing fiction, he likes to teach acting, voice-over and writing workshops. His favorite expression is: "Just tell the damn story."

Writing has become Ken's second life: he has been a Marine, played collegiate football, been a Texas wildcatter, cattle and horse rancher, professional film and TV actor and director, and now...a novelist. Who knew?

Ken Farmer's dialogue flows like a beautiful western river...it's the gold standard...Carole Beers

Web page: www.KenFarmer-Author.net

ISBN-13: - 978-1-7329119-3-2
ISBN-10: - 1-7329119-3-2
Timber Creek Press
Imprint of Timber Creek Productions, LLC
312 N. Commerce St.
Gainesville, Texas 76240

Published by: Timber Creek Press
timbercreekpresss@yahoo.com
www.timbercreekpress.net
Twitter: @pagact
Facebook Book Page:
www.facebook.com/TimberCreekPress
Ken's email: pagact@yahoo.com
214-533-4964

DEDICATION

This tome, is book #15 in the award-winning, The Nations Series, #5 of the spin-off Bone Series and is dedicated to four of my favorite actors from my acting class that I taught for 17 years.

Vivian Jimenez Hall...My visual inspiration for Loraine Bone...Eryn Brooke...My visual inspiration for Inspector Stella Johnson... Brandi D'Aun Price...my inspiration for Peach Presley and Kelly 'Gunny' Jackson for Captain St. John. I love you all.

ACKNOWLEDGMENT

The author gratefully acknowledges Lt. Colonel Clyde DeLoach, USMC (Ret.), Buck Stienke, and novelist Mary Deal for their invaluable help in proofing, beta reading and editing this novel.

This novel is a work of fiction...except the parts that aren't. Names, characters, places and incidents are either the products of the author's imagination or are used fictitiously and sometimes not. Any resemblance to actual persons, living or dead, business establishments, events or locales is entirely coincidental, except where they aren't.

TIMBER CREEK PRESS

PREFACE

BY KEN FARMER - AUTHOR

This story was told to me by a man who I knew for many years and that I trusted completely...I shall call him, 'Padrino'...he is still with us and is one of the characters in this story.

Padrino personally met and interviewed the character I call 'Lucy'...she was an *Anunnaki* alien from the planet I am calling, *Tyrin,* located some thirty-four parsecs—over one hundred and ten light years—across the galaxy in Orion's Arm. Lucy survived the crash of her spaceship on Earth April 17, 1897 near the small Texas town of Aurora. It's known as Texas' Roswell. She was not rescued by her people until 2014.

Her story was originally chronicled in *Legend of Aurora*, written by Buck Stienke and myself and published in 2014.

I was personally acquainted with Darrell Bone and Loraine Rodriguez, although that isn't their real names, which I shall keep secret for sake of their own anonymity and privacy.

I reintroduced 'Lucy' in my historical fiction novel, *Flynn* and further in *Steeldust, Bone, Bone's Law, Bone & Loraine,* and now *Bone's Gold*. She is featured with the Black Eagle Force in *Aurora: Invasion,* also written by Buck Stienke and myself.

You may believe this story or not. I'm satisfied I'm presenting what I know to be true in my mind and, hopefully, in an entertaining fashion...It's up to you.

And this is the way it went...So grab some hair and take a deep seat...

CHAPTER ONE

FLYNN RANCH
1898

Bone, Mason and Padrino were walking Mason and Fiona's new ranch adjacent to the Wilsons in southwestern Cooke County, Texas. They had purchased the full section, 640 acres, from Robert and Suellyn Manier.

"This is the area I saw the Indian artifacts when me and Fiona were first givin' the place a walk...Here and over by that limestone ridge over yonder...arrowheads and spearheads, some obsidian by the way, pottery shards an' the like."

He pointed just the other side of Bone. "That would possibly mean they may have come from New Mexico or Mexico...Somewhere that has volcanos, I'd say."

His eye caught a glint in the morning sun, near his foot. "Hello, what's this?" Bone picked up a gold-looking disk about the size of a silver dollar, partially showing in the dirt. There was a small multifaceted ruby in the center.

Padrino, the nearest to him, stepped over to see what he held. His knees almost buckled when he saw it.

"What's the matter, Padrino? You all right?"

The white-haired, retired Master Gunnery Sergeant squatted down, put one hand on the ground and took several deep breaths. "Just got a little dizzy for a second."

He rose back to a standing position. "Let me see that disk."

Bone brushed the dirt from it and placed it in Padrino's hand. He shook his head. "Wow, got visions like I did the first time Lucy and I touched when we met in 2014."

"I got them, too, first time I touched her right after her ship crashed at Aurora last year," said Mason.

"I also got them when I first held the *moldivite* crystal," commented Padrino.

"What kind of visions did you get from the disk?" asked Bone.

"Barren mountains, small trees beside maize fields in the flatter ground next to them. People surrounding what is apparently a priest or chieftain...He was directing the men of the tribe to pick up some bundles that looked heavy, and then...it was gone."

Padrino looked up at Bone. "They were our ancestors, the *Paracas*, that preceded and became part of the *Nazca* around 100 BC." He looked at Mason and then Bone again. "It was me...I was the priest."

"How do you know?" He shook his head.

"I just know, Bone...I just know."

Padrino turned and walked directly, almost as if in a trance, to a large, almost fifty-foot high limestone outcrop and pointed. "There...Remove those rocks at the base."

Bone and Mason lifted and moved various rocks from where they were piled against the cliff face.

Behind the rocks was a hand-carved niche in the rock. Padrino stepped up and helped pull the rest of the smaller rocks away and knelt down in front of the three foot high cavity that was about two feet wide and two feet deep.

There was a glint of light from inside when a cloud that had been obscuring the sun moved on past. Padrino pulled his smart phone out, turned on its LED light and shined it inside.

In the center of the alcove stood a golden statue over eighteen inches tall. It looked like it had some type of helmet with radiating spires coming out from it, and there was a large disk with at least an eight thousand carat ruby embedded in the center, identical to the small one in Padrino's hand—hung on a thick gold chain about its neck.

"An effigy of the *Anunnaki*..."

BONE'S GOLD

WILSON RANCH

Bone, Padrino and Bone's bride, Loraine, were sitting in ladderback, calf-hide seat rockers on the wide, wraparound porch, sipping on morning coffee.

"Padrino, I get a strong sense from you that you have more reason to stay than just liking the simplicity of the time here."

"You're getting too good at that, Bone," he replied.

"Good at what?" asked Loraine.

Padrino took a sip of the hot Arbuckles brew. "Reading other people's thoughts like Lucy."

Bone chuckled. "No, not even close. She was reading me in detail over a hundred miles away, remember?…I'm just getting a feeling is all."

"Well, it's close enough. When I figured out how I could control the electromagnetic vortex we were transported through in the cave with my *moldivite* crystal…thought it might be a good time to check out a legend."

"About what?" asked Bone.

"You know about our heritage from the *Nazca* people of Peru on your father's mother's side...my sister?"

"You've told me some about that."

"One of the things I've never bothered to tell you about was the gold treasure our sect of the *Nazca* took out of Peru during a disagreement with another tribal chieftain somewhere around 100 BC, that I mentioned earlier...They developed about the same time as the *Maya*, but weren't nearly as sophisticated...They also traded with the *Maya* and the *Aztec*."

"Oh, this is getting interesting...go on," said the raven-haired Loraine, leaning forward in her chair.

"The gold technology of the *Nazca* was of the cold-hammered type, they hadn't learned smelting, so every artifact they created was almost pure gold..."

"Pure enough it was shaped into what they wanted...by just hammering," interrupted Bone. "Like that statue we found yesterday."

"Correct. Almost ninety-nine percent pure...There were representations of animals, offerings to their god, even, I was told as a child, a statue of the aliens that visited them...as we saw."

"They built the lines and geoglyphs in the desert to honor them," added Loraine. "They looked upon them as gods."

"Yes, they built them to signal us to come back and somewhat of a homage thing that we told them wasn't necessary," the diminutive 4'10" stranded *Anunnaki* alien, *Annuna*—named Lucy by Mason's wife, Deputy US Marshal Fiona Miller Flynn—said as she came out the screen door with her own coffee.

"You and I will have this discussion in 2014, Lucy. We discussed this and many other things for hours and hours," commented Padrino.

"I'm sure we will, you are fascinating to visit with…much as *Anompoli Lawa*. You and he both understand the esoteric value of our visits to your early ancestors. We quit showing ourselves over a thousand of your years ago."

Padrino grinned. "You mentioned how you pretended to be a mute abandoned child until you were adopted by the Wilsons, not long after your ship crashed…We discussed, or will discus, the pyramids in Egypt and the temples of *Puma Punku*…How you used your inertialess anti-gravitational technology to move those monstrous, multi-ton, blocks of stone."

"Loraine and I will get to fly one of your inertialess drive spacecraft fighters in 2014 in the battle against the *Reptoids* invasion."**

Awesome...I think you put it that at the speeds you travel and maneuver, without the inertialess drive...you would be so much Tyranian goo on the first change of direction or acceleration."

***Aurora: Invasion - (Black Eagle Force Book 6) - 2014*

"Yes, I'm sure we will talk about that, but what's this *Nazcan* gold you were mentioning, Padrino?...We had them mine gold for us for several hundred years. We use it in our electronics and in our drive systems...Gold is a neutral element that functions to keep the matter and antimatter separated."

"Our ancestors had accumulated quite a lot of pure gold artifacts that two of the sects squabbled over and the one Bone and I descended from took all they could carry and went north."

"North is a long direction, my Padrino. Any other leads?" asked Bone.

"I'm getting there. The legend goes, they traveled all the way to North America passing through the *Maya* and the *Aztec* territories because of their trade relations."

"North America...Big place," said Bone.

Lucy got a wry grin on her face.

"More specifically, what is now Texas and even more specifically...the Brazos River valley in Palo Pinto County..."

"Which is underneath Possum Kingdom Lake, in our time...*Voilà*," exclaimed Bone. "And that's where that effigy came from?"

"That's my thinking, yes...It could have been a single family or possibly even more to move up here closer to the Red River...or it could be they picked a cave in the Brazos River valley to store most of their treasure...then scattered so they would be hard to track down."

"My question is, why didn't you bring the statue back here instead leaving it and covering the little alcove back up?" asked Loraine as she held her cup with both hands on the chilly December morning.

"It's best not to disturb an archeological find until an expert can document it. We need to send a letter to the science department at North Texas Normal College in Denton...see if they have an archeologist or an antiquities expert on staff who can come up here and verify our find before anybody touches it," said Padrino. "It's known as The University of North Texas in our time."

"Oh, why didn't you say so...I've taken some classes there," replied Loraine.

"I just did."

"My sweet Double D is a little slow sometimes, Padrino," said Bone. "That's why she still goes to school."

"Damn you, Bone." She gave the 6'8" big man her I'm going to hurt you look.

He winked at her. "Yes, dear." He remembered Cletus' advice to him, Bodie, and Mason about the secret to a long and happy marriage was just two words.

"Let me see that picture you took, Padrino," asked Lucy.

He swiped his phone on and touched the Gallery icon. The picture of the statue was the first one. He handed it to Lucy.

She studied it for a moment, and then nodded. "That is somewhat like the suits we wore back then. The antennae weren't quite that tall, though."

"What about that giant ruby?" asked Bone. "It looks like the same...size and all...that we saw on your spacesuits in 2014."

"Then you know it's not a real ruby...We manufacture them and call it *seatonite*, and no gemologist on Tellus would be able to tell the difference."

"What does it do differently?" asked Padrino.

"A natural ruby is made up of hexagonal scalenohedron crystals."

"Come again?" asked Mason.

Lucy smiled. "It's a twelve-sided polyhedron, and each of its faces is an identical scalene triangle, or a triangle with three different side lengths...although with uneven bottom edges."

"Uh-huh." Mason had a glazed look come across his eyes.

Lucy grinned again. "Our crystals are also hexagonal scalenohedron... but, all perfectly uniform...and, now here's the real difference. Rather than being aligned randomly as in nature, they are perfectly aligned together...vertically."

Bone shook his head. "Not getting your point, Lucy."

"Long ago, our scientists learned to align the crystals in a vertical configuration...with the negatively charged ends all facing outward."

"Which means?" asked Padrino.

"It means they act as a funnel or like a flue or channel to draw in the powerful cosmic rays into the accumulator...Power, in other words...That statue you found with that size stone can generate an enormous amount of energy," said Lucy.

Padrino looked deep in thought for a moment, reached in one of the deep side pockets of his BDUs, pulled out the translucent green crystal and held it up. "I'll bet anything that my *moldivite* crystal is the same."

"How do you mean, Padrino?" asked Lucy.

"Normal *moldivite* molecules are amorphous, and not repeated like a natural crystal because it doesn't grow...it was formed on tremendous impact by a large meteorite...Each and every one of the molecules are different, like snowflakes, because part of it is terrestrial and part is extraterrestrial...but in this case, I think that each of the 'snowflakes' is in order...facing in one direction, like your *seatonite*."

"And that's what gave it the power to amplify your zen energy to enter the electromagnetic vortex," said Lucy.

"Correct...I believe I'll keep this in my pocket...Never know when a vortex will flux along this ley line we're on."

"Good idea, Padrino," commented Bone. "Might make even one of our cell phones work."

Loraine held out her hand. "May I see that picture."

Lucy passed the smart phone for her perusal of the photo. "That's very interesting...Seems like I've seen something similar on a web site about the Inca's I was looking at one time."

She handed the phone back to Padrino.

"We visited the *Inca* along with the *Maya, Aztec* and at *Tiahuanaco* before them...They called us *Viracocha*...God of action, shaper of many worlds and destroyer of many worlds." She shook her head, ruffling her three-inch long brown, pixie cut, hair style.

Padrino got to his feet and headed to the door. "Going after a warm-up?" asked Bone.

"Nope, going to write another letter to Stella and Peach...They're good enough investigators that I'll

15

bet they will continue to search through the desk for more letters. There's four more of those small receipt drawers in the top…Besides, I smell Mary Lou baking cinnamon rolls." He had a big grin across his face.

"Taught those girls everything I know," said Bone.

"Took you all of ten minutes, huh, dear?" quipped Loraine.

"Twelve," he retorted. "It was like trying to get a drink from a fire hose."

"Oh, my Lord," commented Loraine. She turned to Padrino. "You talk like they'll get it tomorrow."

"Well, could be it's like Einstein said, 'the past, present and future may all exist at the same time…as part and parcel of the quantum entanglement theorem…Spooky action at a distance'," added Padrino. "Plus, need to write that letter to North Texas Normal College."

"You're handier than handles on a jug, Padrino. Glad you joined us," said Bone.

"Figured that no matter where you were…there you are and you needed some help."

§§§

CHAPTER TWO

GAINESVILLE PD
2018

Peach Presley, the forensics technician, was at Bone's desk in the office occupied by the detectives and investigators. She was doing additional Google searches on Bone, Loraine and Padrino in case she and Stella Johnson had missed something out at

Bone's ranch where they were house and dog sitting.

"Stella, Stella, Stella," she shouted as she jumped up and down in her chair.

"I'm sitting right here at Loraine's desk, Peach, no need to shout...Good gosh," the 5'2" blond bombshell with antique gold-eyes, replied.

"Look, look, I declare, this is gonna blow your dress up, sweetie," her 5'10" attractive brunette, best friend from Georgia said. "On the eighth day, God created search engines."

"I do wish you'd speak English sometime, girlfriend," Stella said as she rolled her chair over to look at Peach's monitor.

"Sugah, it's like that cute Winston Churchill said...'The most beautiful voice in the world is that of an educated Southern woman'...an' Cutie Pie, you know I've got more degrees than Carter's got liver pills."

Stella grinned. "Well, you are sweet, not to say anything about being smart."

"Baby doll, I was raised on sweet tea and a whole bunch of Jesus...Now cast your peepers on that." She pointed at her screen.

Stella leaned over and squinted her eyes at the aged, faded, pixelated, newspaper page on the screen.

"It's from the Rosston Weekly Chronicle, December 28, 1898."

"*Stella and Peach...Look for...Look for...fur.* That's all I can make out...fur, fur...Further!"

"I do believe you're right, Sweet Pea."

They looked at each other and simultaneously said, "More letters!"

"I mind we'll just have to wait till we cut it to see if it's a red meat or yellow," commented Peach.

"Do what?"

"Gotta wait till we go back out to the house, Buttercup." Peach glanced over at Stella. "You're grinnin' like a possum eatin' 'simmons."

"You just tickle me to death, sometimes."

"I know...most of the time I can't even stand my ownself..." She giggled. "Reckon we need to go tell the Captain, directly."

"Does that mean now?"

Peach got a big grin across her face. "Honey, it means when I can get you to be calm and act like a Southern belle...You know how he gets when we go in actin' like two rats in a drain pipe."

"Right."

"I say let's wait till we go out to the house an' see as we can find what Padrino's talkin' about...Then go in waltzin' in his office. Less chance of him pitchin' a hissy fit for bein' half-ass in our jobs."

WILSON RANCH
1898

"Get 'er done?" asked Bone as Padrino came back out on the porch with a fresh cup of coffee.

"I'd say...Going to have to find some other hidin' places. They'll be finding letters I haven't sent yet."

"Huh?" inquired Mason. "Don't follow. How can they find a letter or letters you haven't sent yet?"

"Because they're in the future and all the letters I will ever send are already there, but I haven't sent them yet...See?"

"Yeah...No."

"It is kind of hard to get your head around, but I see what Padrino's talking about. Like *Anompoli*

Lawa said, 'If you go to the past, then you are part of the past...and always have been," said Loraine.

"So, you're sayin' that Padrino could have found his own letters in that rolltop before he came here because he had sent them a hundred and twenty years earlier...but didn't know it?" said Mason.

"Well, like I always say...When you don't know that you don't know...it's a whole lot different than when you know that you don't know...until you know it," commented Bone. "In other words, you don't know what you don't know until you find out you don't know."

"I think I like what Padrino said better," said Mason.

Lucy giggled. "Not to worry, gentlemen. The greatest minds on two worlds haven't totally gotten a grasp on the paradoxes of time travel yet. That's why I said that *Anompoli Lawa's* explanation was one of the best and simplest I'd ever heard."

"The wisdom of the Amerindian Shamans is not to ever be taken lightly. I firmly believe they have a direct pipeline to the netherworlds when needed, or to the great Creator himself," commented Padrino.

"In the millennia we've been coming to Tellus, I've never ceased to be amazed at the different names that are attributed to the Creator…From the Egyptian *Aten* or *Ra,* to Judea's *Elohim, Yahweh, Jehovah, Jesus*…the Amerindians, *Chí-hóo-wah, Great Spirit,* Muslims, *Allah,* to our *Great Entity*…when they're all referring to the same Creator…And the fact that the different societies actually fight and kill one another over which one is correct…and they're all the same." Lucy shook her head in wonder. "It's like three monkeys fighting over three identical bananas."

"Lucy, that's the best simile to explain religion I've ever heard," commented Padrino. "May I borrow it?"

"Of course, it's not mine to lend…it's the truth and the truth always belongs to all."

"It's a shame that so many of the so-called men of God or men of the cloth pass their own twisted interpretation of the various texts, claiming them to be direct words from God." Padrino took a sip of the stout brew. "When, for example, at the Council of Nicaea in 325 AD, a group of old men got together at the behest of an unbaptized, atheist, emperor, Constantine I, and argued over what texts or books would or would not go into the New Testament Bible with the Torah, and even changing the translations to suit their own proclivities." He got to his feet and pitched the grounds in the yard. "…and then had the gall to call it The Holy Word," said Padrino.

"You have to wade through the chaff to find the wheat…but it's there," added Bone.

"That's like the little boy trapped in a room full of horse manure digging frantically…Not to get out, but to find the pony that he knew had to be there," said Loraine.

Lucy nodded at her. "Another great simile."

"The *Anunnaki* try to take a common sense approach to the *Great Entity*.

Fiona had joined the others on the porch and caught the gist of the conversations. "This all reminds me of my favorite quote from Shakespeare: 'There are more things in heaven and earth, Horatio, Than are dreamt of in your philosophy.'…Hamlet."

"When you boil it down…it's all about power," said Padrino. "All about power."

Bone looked up. "Well, since we're jumping in here with quotes…Here's mine: 'Power tends to corrupt, and absolute power corrupts absolutely.

Great men are almost always bad men,'...John Dalberg-Acton."

"He also said, 'There are two things which cannot be attacked in front...ignorance and narrow-mindedness. They can only be shaken by the simple development of the contrary qualities. They will not bear discussion'," added Padrino.

"You think that's why your ancestor's sect broke away from the *Nazca* civilization...that he felt they were dealing with ignorance and narrow mindedness?" asked Lucy.

"That's my thinking," answered Padrino.

"I saw something written by the western writer, Ken Farmer, from what he calls his *Ponderings*... 'Wisdom grows in direct ratio to one's awareness of his own ignorance'."

"True, Bone...maybe the priest or chieftain I saw in my vision became aware of their own ignorance and to paraphrase Lord Acton again...'stupidity and ignorance are constantly on the march...They can't be stopped, only avoided'," added Padrino.

"Once the preponderance of your population on Tellus understands that simple precept, then you'll finally make progress in the area of humanity over industrialism…and have a place in the Federation of Planets."

"You mean there is such a thing?" asked Loraine. "Like on *Star Trek*?"

"Oh, most certainly. I'm not sure what that '*Star Trek*' you mentioned is, but, there is a Federation of Planets."

"*Star Trek* is one of those play-acting shows they put on moving pictures. It's called science fiction…like H.G. Wells and Jules Vern," added Bone.

Padrino turned to Lucy. "You will tell me in 2014 that you thought the creator of *Star Trek*, Gene Roddenberry, actually met with some of your people in the 1950s and many of his ideas on the show came from the *Anunnaki*."

"I'm sure that's possible, but to me, it hasn't happened yet…but it is often how we do things. We give certain people pieces of information to gradually expose your society to those ideas, so it won't be such a shock when they actually see them." She paused and looked out across the rolling hills toward the wooded creek.

"I do know that we've met with your Nikola Tesla with certain ideas involving electromagnetic wave and vibration science…All physical matter has its own vibratory wave."

"Is that one reason you had some of the early people mine gold for you…for it's shielding effects on other vibratory wave lengths," asked Padrino.

"Yes, we use a lot of it in our electronics and drive systems, as I have mentioned. We had accumulated all we will need for a long time by the turn of the last millennium. By then, the people that mined it for us had also found many uses for it because it was so malleable and didn't corrode."

"You helped them learn about art, beauty, creativity and decoration."

"And the cause of many deaths over the shiny yellow metal," added Mason. "It makes men crazy sometimes."

"One big reason for keeping the news about the statue quiet…It will bring the ne'er-do-wells and malefactors out of the woodworks," said Fiona. "Good idea, Padrino…to keep it close to your vest."

The venerable retired Marine nodded. "It will bring the treasure hunters to this area like over around Superstition Mountain in Arizona…and that always brings thieves, gamblers and prostitutes."

"Like all those people looking for the Seven Cities of Gold and the Lost City of Cibola," commented Bone.

"But, aren't those just myths?" inquired Fiona. "Like Atlantis."

"That's what they thought about the city of Troy from the Greek legends...and Homer's, *The Iliad* and *The Odyssey*...Until it was discovered in 1868," said Padrino. "It'll almost be completely excavated in our time...So who knows?"

"Do you think we can trust whatever scientist or archeologists the college will send over?" asked Loraine.

"Probably not, but, I've got some plans to help out there," answered Padrino.

§§§

CHAPTER THREE

NORTH TEXAS NORMAL COLLEGE
1898

"Who's the letter from Hermie?" asked Doctor Maywether of the English Department as he poured himself a cup of coffee in the staff lounge.

Professor Herman Cobb of the Archeology Department looked up from where he was perusing the letter at one of the tables.

The slight-built, middle-aged, balding professor, two years from tenure, cleared his throat. "Oh, just a request from some rancher by the name of Jethro Pereira up in Cooke County wanting some find certified."

"Pereira? That's Portuguese isn't it?"

"Damn if I know, country's filling up with foreigners."

"You going?"

"Oh, I suppose there's an outside chance one of these immigrants has found something. Seriously doubt it. Never heard of anything of any substance being found in north Texas, besides the usual arrowheads and pottery."

"No Indian mounds?" asked Maywether.

"Not of any import. What there were from the *Caddo* were dug up long ago…Found a few fresh water pearls most likely from down along the Concho River and some at Lake Caddo near Marshal in northeast Texas…It's the only natural lake in Texas. Believed to have been formed by the New Madrid earthquake in 1811." He got to his feet.

Would they be considered an antiquity?" asked Maywether.

"Not from the lake, but when the area all the way over to what is now Louisiana was swampy, it produced fresh water pearls for hundreds of years."

"Fresh water pearls? You mentioned them before...I didn't know they were valuable."

Cobb snickered. "Oh, very valuable. The *Atakapan* and *Caddo* Indians dealt in them heavily...traded in them. They were their *wampum*...There were white pearls from washboard mussels, pink pearls from white-eye mussels, and the most unusual of all, were wine and blue pearls from buttermilk mussels from that swampy area that's under the lake now."

"Could those be more valuable, then?" asked the English professor.

"Now, that could be a bird of a different feather...Could be very valuable. Much more so than salt water pearls. But, once the lake was formed they became almost impossible to find, so people quit trying."

"Where do you have to go?"

"Take the train up to Gainesville, they're picking me up in a buckboard or something, I imagine...I'm certainly not riding a horse out to some godforsaken wilderness location." He folded the letter and stuffed it in the inside pocket of his jacket.

"Where're you headed?" asked Maywether.

"Down to the Longhorn Saloon for a beer...You want to come?"

"Thanks, but I think not...Have essays to grade before class tomorrow. Be thankful you're not tenured yet. Have to toe the mark a little more...Have one for me."

An hour later, Professor Cobb walked into the dimly lit Odysseus Saloon. It was several levels above a backwater saloon out in the smaller towns.

There was a stage for live shows, barber shop quartets, and local bands to play on the weekend. Plus, a better than average kitchen for a usually large lunch crowd and a growing clientele for the evening meal.

He sauntered over to the bar where the bartender asked for his order, "What'll it be, Professor, the usual beer?"

"Actually, Charles, I think I'll have a sour mash."

"Comin' right up." He set a four ounce gill tumbler in front of the professor and then filled it almost to the top with a good quality Kentucky sour mash.

Herman took a slow sip and savored the taste. "Mmm, that's quite smooth, my man, quite smooth." He downed the balance of the glass. "Let's have another."

Charles filled his glass again. "Better be careful there Professor, that stuff can sneak up on a man…Especially if he's not used to it."

"I can handle my spirits, my good man…I can assure you." He downed the second glass.

A well-dressed man sidled up next to the professor at the bar after he and a couple of friends came through the batwing doors. "What are you having, friend?"

"A very good Kentucky sour mash, sir, and you?"

"Believe I'll have the same…Give me what he's having, and fill his glass while you're at it, Charlie."

"Uh…All right." He set another gill liquor glass on the bar and filled them both.

The well-dressed man laid a couple of dollars on the bar, picked up his glass and nodded at the professor. "To you, sir. May your life continue with clear skies and fair wind."

They clinked glasses. The professor downed most of his and the other gentleman only took a sip.

"How would you like to join my friends and me in a friendly game of chance over at our table?"

"Well, I don't know..."

"Come now, we're all friends here..." He turned to the bartender. "Freshen up his drink and bring it, along with one for Lawrence and Howard, over to our regular table...if you would?"

He took Herman's elbow and led him over to a round table with two other also well-dressed men. "Here, have a seat, sir...We're having a gentlemen's game of stud. Only a dollar to get in...Ah, here's our drinks...Sit, sit," he said as Charlie set the drinks on the table with a bit of a frown.

An hour later, a very drunk Professor Herman Cobb patted his pockets. "Gads, I don't seem to have any money left, my friends. But, it's been a splendid game and I must go…The little wife awaits." He started to rise and the first man put his hand on his forearm.

"I'm sorry, Professor, but you owe the table two hundred dollars…And we expect what is owed to us…I doubt the 'little wife' will be very happy with you."

SANTA FE DEPOT
GAINESVILLE, TEXAS

The big black, coal-fired locomotive hissed to a stop from the south, blowing out a big cloud of steam from her relief valves at the red brick platform outside the depot a little past sunrise. The morning train to Oklahoma City arrived in Gainesville at 8 AM.

Bone, Loraine and Padrino were standing in the disembarking area for passengers, scanning the people getting off the train for a likely academic type.

"Dollar to a donut that fellow getting off the second car in the brown bowler and brown houndstooth three piece suit is our man," said Bone.

"No bet," replied Padrino.

None of them noticed the three men in nondescript western trail clothes standing under the eaves of the depot, smoking qurleys and also watching the passengers getting off the train.

Padrino stepped up to the mousy man carrying a small leather valise. "Professor Cobb?"

"Mister Pereira, I assume?"

"Who?…Oh, right. Just call me Padrino, please."

Herman nodded. "Mister Padrino."

"No, no mister…Just Padrino."

"Fine, you can call me Hermie…Short for Herman."

"Would have never guessed," muttered Bone under his breath to Loraine.

"This is my godson, Bone and his wife, Loraine."

He looked appraisingly at Loraine and smiled, and then up at the big man. "Uh…Mister and Missus Bone. Pleased, I'm sure."

"That all you have with you?" Padrino indicated the valise.

"It is…Figured I would catch the 7 PM train back to Denton. You have a carriage, I presume?"

"This way, sir," said Bone.

"So, tell me what do you think you've found?" asked the professor.

"Well, you can tell us. We believe it's maybe some type of Incan artifact," answered Padrino.

"Well, I sincerely doubt it...Not this far north. Incan artifacts have not been found north of the Yucatan...to my knowledge."

Faye Skeans' two-horse black Phaeton was tied to the iron hitching post in front of the depot.

"Let me have your satchel, Professor," said Bone.

"It's all right, I'll just hold it," Hermie commented as he clambered aboard on the left side.

Padrino stepped up to the driver's side on the right, while Bone untied the lead from the post and hooked it back to the harness.

After mounting his big black, seventeen hand, half-Frisian gelding, Hildebrandt, and Loraine, her sorrel, blaze-face, mare, Sweet Face, they led out toward California Street and turned west.

A short way just past the edge of town, Padrino reined the matched set of Saddlebreds to a halt.

"I'm afraid we're going to have to ask you to wear this blindfold, Hermie. If we have what we think we have, we want to keep the location secret…I'm sure you understand," said Padrino.

The professor appeared very concerned as he glanced around the carriage. "Well, I don't know, I've never had to do anything like this, I assure you," he nervously replied.

"Have no fear, Professor Cobb, my wife and I are both sheriff's deputies and are along for your protection," commented Bone.

"Unusual to see a woman deputy…But, uh…in order to properly certify your find, I must know its location, you understand."

Loraine nodded. "Times are changing, Professor."

"I suppose," he replied.

"That will be no problem, sir…once we determine what we do have…We're afraid it could cause somewhat of a stir and would like to be prepared," said Padrino.

A slight look of relief came over the man's face, coloring his pallor somewhat—but not completely.

Behind the carriage, on the east side of the Elm Fork of the Trinity, the three men from the saloon shielded themselves behind some of the heavy brush, mostly cedar, bordering the creek.

"Wonder what they're doin' that for?" asked Johnson Kittleson, the man who first approached the professor in the saloon as he watched Padrino tie the bandana around Cobb's eyes.

"Apparently your instincts were on spot about getting that Professor Maywether from the English department at the college in your pocket, Kittleson…Nobody calls a archeologist out to look at arrowheads," answered Lawrence Clagett, a somewhat dark complexioned man with equally dark eyes and waxed mustache.

"Those professor idiots had no business gambling with us, but it's going to turn out advantageous in the end…owing us a little over a thousand dollars, now. One way or another," added Howard Parker.

The three grifters reined out in the road, keeping well back from the carriage.

"Following their tracks will be simple," said Clagett. "The tires of that carriage are much more narrow than a buckboard."

Once Cobb was blindfolded securely, Padrino flicked the reins over the two sorrel gelding's rumps. "Come up there, boys."

He clicked his tongue twice and headed the team in the direction of the small town of Era.

It was almost twenty miles to the property where the gold statue was.

Kittlson, Clagett and Parker rode out of sight over a mile back, following the tracks of the carriage.

§§§

CHAPTER FOUR

BONE'S RANCH
2018

"Turn the drawer over," suggested Stella after Peach had pulled the first receipt drawer out on the left side and found nothing behind it.

"Ah...Looky here...Well, I'm mud an' magnolias," said Peach. "He stuck it to the bottom with some of that sealin' wax...Don't that beat all?"

She handed the yellowed paper to Stella. "Your turn, Darlin."

Police Inspector Johnson carefully unfolded the brittle stationary. "It's a map with some notes and directions."

"Are you goin' to read 'em or do you need some help?"

Stella glanced over at her friend. "Just looking at the map…'*Lovely Ladies*…Aw, how nice…*I'm assuming you found the letter as well as the other one and have secured the property for us.*

If you'll follow the map which leads to a limestone cliff facing north on that property and then follow it to approximately the center. There you will see a pile of rocks that fell from the face in the further past. Remove them and you'll find a small, hand-carved notch in the face of the cliff with a gold statue of Lucy's people inside.

We left it hidden as we felt it could become compromised in this time period. Near as we could tell, it dates from around 100 BC, or earlier.

Remove it and place it in the cellar with the box of what remains of the gold and diamonds. See you soon, maybe. Padrino, Bone and Loraine, PS, We've got an archeologist coming up in a couple of days from North Texas Normal College to certify the find.'...Well, I'll be," Stella muttered and looked at Peach again.

They grabbed each others hands and jumped up and down, squealing like school girls.

They stopped and Stella got a puzzled expression on her face. "What's North Texas Normal College?"

"Oh, Hon, that's what they used to call The University of North Texas when it started up...Means they mostly trained high school grads to be teachers."

Stella looked a little embarrassed. "I knew that."

"Uh-huh...Bless your heart."

"Well, what say we go get Bone's Gator out of the barn and run over there?"

"If you're waitin' on me, you're backin' up, Babe."

Fifteen minutes after grabbing some lunch, they opened the doors to the big red barn. They checked the gas on the green beast that was parked next to the pristine sky blue, 1930 L-29 Coupe Cord with original style wide white sidewalls and twin spares mounted on the twelve inch wide running boards Lucy had given Bone and let Tyrin jump into the back of the big four wheeler. Peach fired it up and they accelerated out of the barn headed east.

"Think we can get across Black Creek this time of year?" asked Stella.

"Fixin' to find out...Button up, buttercup," Peach said in a terrible Betty Davis imitation, from *All About Eve*—that sounded more like Vivian Leigh from *Gone With the Wind*. "...it's gonna be a bumpy ride...I'm gonna let the hammer down an' air this son of a gun out...Bet they haven't driven it since bully was a pup."

Stella zipped up, buttoned the top of her dark brown leather bomber jacket and pulled up her collar. "Let her rip." She slipped a pink scrunchie on her long blond tresses and pulled them back into a low ponytail.

Tyrin stood on his back feet, draped his front paws over Stella's shoulders and leaned out to the side to catch the wind. His lips fluttered in the breeze as Peach raced the Gator across the brown winter-killed prairie grass.

SOUTHWESTERN COOKE COUNTY

Bone and Loraine continued to lead southwest in the general direction of Rosston. They paused for a moment and let Padrino catch up.

"Gonna check on something, Padrino, catch up with you," said Bone.

His godfather smiled knowingly, nodded and clicked the team back up into a road trot as Bone wheeled Hildebrandt to the north and over the nearest hill. Loraine reined Sweet Face to the south.

"Are Mister and Missus Bone going somewhere?" asked the blindfolded Cobb as he heard the horses gallop off.

"Going to see a man about a dog, I imagine."

"Oh, right…May have to do that myself in a bit."

"Let me know."

The cool Texas winter morning caused the professor to snug his mackinaw tighter about his neck as the carriage moved along the rutted ranch road.

After circling back about mile and a half, Bone approached the road from the north through the cedar trees and other brush while Loraine came in from the south. They caught sight of each other and signaled.

Both reined their mounts behind some thick copses of juniper, laden with the season's purple berries, that hid them well from the road, and waited.

It was only a short couple of moments until the three con-artists trotted into view from around a turn in the road.

Bone nodded at Loraine and she walked her mare out in the middle of the road, turned the horse to face the men and stopped.

"What's all this then?" asked Kittleson. "Who are you?"

Even though he recognized her from the Santa Fe Depot, he pretended he didn't know who she was.

"Deputy Sheriff Loraine Bone…and you?"

"Well, not that it's any of your business, woman, we're just passin' through," said, Parker.

He was the only one dressed like a gunhawk and wore his Colt in a low crossdraw.

"You may call me Deputy, but not 'woman'…clear?"

"Haw! You sayin' you're not a woman?" asked the gunman.

"No, not at all…But, when you say it with an obvious lack of respect…it makes a difference."

"Well, be a man or a woman, I don't give a damn…You got a smart mouth on you." He started side-passing his gelding to the edge of the road to create distance between him and the other two.

"Move that horse another foot and you'll be looking up at the sky…but not seeing anything," Loraine said.

"You don't seem to count very well…woman. They's three of us an' one of you."

"Just about even odds…I make it." She grinned at the hatchet-faced gunman.

Parker reached across and palmed his Colt, but before it cleared leather, the very air shook with a horrendous explosion. A cloud of red mist blossomed around the gunhawk's chest as he flipped backward out of his saddle throwing both arms up in the air—he was dead before he hit the ground.

Bone walked his horse out of the cover, still holding his Smith & Wesson 500 in his right hand. "She tried to give you boys a chance to be gentlemen...but apparently you weren't having any of it."

"You shot him in cold blood," yelled Clagett.

"Nope. If you'll look, you'll see his Colt is laying beside him in the dirt, hammer's still cocked...and now take a gander at my sweet wife. She's holding what's called a semiautomatic .45 in her hand. I shot before she could...Saving the two of you idiot's lives."

"What do you mean?" asked Kittleson.

"Oh, she wouldn't have stopped with your running buddy there on the ground...She would have killed the three of you. Just on general principles and because you were together...Isn't that right, Hon?"

"Pretty close, Dear," Loraine replied sweetly.

"She's got this thing about being disrespected, you see...Doesn't tolerate it." He chuckled. "Have to watch her like a hawk."

"Oh, Honey, that's not true...Only some of the time." She blushed a little.

Bone looked at her and then at Clagett and Kittleson. "We just took out the Rudabaugh gang over in Jacksboro last week...all twelve of them. She shot three just for looking cross-eyed at her."

Loraine was doing her best not to grin.

"The Rudabaugh gang?...From New Mexico?" said Lawrence.

"Yep...They weren't being nice at all." Bone looked at Loraine. "That was the only bunch we killed that day, wasn't it, Sweetheart?"

"That was all, Darling...just those twelve."

Lawrence and Johnson exchanged glances and made sure their hands were both covering their saddlehorns—as far as possible from their guns.

"What the hell kind of gun is that, anyway?" asked Clagett.

"It's a S&W .50 caliber...the largest, most powerful handgun in the world."

"Gawdawmighty," said Clagett.

"Now, I'd suggest you load stupid there on his horse and take him back to Gainesville to the undertakers...You don't want her to tell you that, believe me," commented Bone as he holstered his hand cannon.

"If we see you following us again, we won't be so generous," said Loraine as she did the same with her Kimber.

"But, we weren't..."

Loraine wagged her finger at Kittleson interrupting him. "Ahh, ahh, ahh...Not nice to try to fool Deputy Bone."

The two men stepped down, picked up Parker's body and slung him, belly down, over his saddle.

"I'd tie his hands and feet together or you're liable to be doing that again a couple of times before you get back to Gainesville, because I want to see you hurry...Understand? Don't walk," added Bone.

He and Loraine watched as the two men tied Parker's hands to his knees under the horse's stomach with his own rope, mount up and gallop back down the road.

They continued to watch until the two were out of sight before they turned to each other and burst out laughing.

"Wish you'd tell me when you're going to start pulling Bone on the bad guys...Thought I was going to burst at the seams." Loraine giggled.

"Well, for future reference, Love, you can always safely count on it...Be ready." His grin spread across his face.

Almost two miles down the road to the southwest, Professor Cobb turned his head in the direction of Padrino. "Was that gunfire? Sounded like a really big gun."

"Believe so...Probably just some hunter out shootin' varmints."

§§§

CHAPTER FIVE

BONE RANCH
2018

Peach drove into Black Creek at a greatly reduced speed from what they were making over the pasture coming up to the waterway.

The clear, slow moving branch crept up the sides of the all-terrain vehicle until the top of the water covered the floorboards. The girls lifted their feet and put them on the dash in front of them. Peach let the versatile four-wheeler creep forward at idle throttle.

The cold water reached the bottom of the seat and kept slowly climbing as the Gator passed the midpoint. Peach and Stella exchanged nervous glances, while Tyrin looked down at the surface almost up to his perch in the small bed behind the seat and whined.

"I'm not crazy about getting my butt wet, girlfriend...especially not in ice cold water," said Stella.

"Me neither, honey bear," Peach replied.

The four heavy-treaded balloon mud tires churned through the chilly liquid on the rock bottom as it pulled the vehicle slowly toward the opposite bank. The water level began to recede more as they neared the other side.

Finally the tires lugged them up on the shore, allowing the water to drain out of the flat floorboard. They put their feet back down and Peach gave the versatile piece of ranch equipment more gas and quickly accelerated back up to speed.

"Well, sweetie, don't know about you, but my pucker string was starting to draw up some," said Peach in relief.

Stella shook her head and managed a grin. "You think?" She pointed off to the north. "I think that's the limestone cliff Padrino has on the map."

"Well, gimme some sugah…If that isn't it, child, it's goin' to miss a good chance."

Peach braked the machine near what they could guess was approximately the center of the ridge and killed the engine. Tyrin jumped down and ran around in circles for a moment.

"Think Tyrin is happy we got here?"

FLYNN RANCH
1898

They had been on the ranch for almost ten minutes when Padrino reined the team to a halt near the outcrop.

"Well, we're here," he said as he leaned over and removed the bandana from the professor's face.

The man blinked and rubbed both eyes for a moment before he looked around.

"I assume you found no structures or remnants of foundations of any kind?"

"Not a thing…Just a small hand-carved alcove." Padrino stepped down from the carriage. "This way Hermie."

Bone and Loraine tied their mounts to a nearby mesquite tree where they immediately began browsing on the seed pods scattered about the ground from the previous summer's production.

Padrino, Loraine and Cobb, followed Bone over to the cliff face to the rocks still piled at the base.

"Ya'll smell something, Padrino?"

The venerable retired Marine sniffed the air as did Loraine.

Padrino looked at Bone with a puzzled expression. "Exhaust?"

"Yes, exhaust," added Loraine.

"Well, if I'm crazy, then we all are." He sniffed again. "Gone now."

"That was odd," said Loraine, as she looked around. "There's no way there could be engine exhaust out here…especially in this time."

"I don't understand what you all are saying," said Cobb.

"It's nothing, Professor. Nothing at all," replied Bone.

He, Loraine and Padrino began removing the rocks and placing them to the side in a semi-neat pile until the top of the opening showed.

"Let me take it from here...if you don't mind," said the professor.

BONE RANCH
2018

"You hear something?" asked Stella.

Peach cocked her head and listened, and then looked all around. "Well, hush my mouth if I don't...Voices. I know I heard voices, but there's nowhere close anybody could be."

Tyrin was running back and forth in front of the cliff, whining and sniffing the air.

"He hears and smells something, too," said Stella.

The Pit Bull ran over to the pile of rocks at the base of the outcrop, whined and looked back at the girls. Then he spun around three times, jumped up in the air and barked.

"I s'wanie, he used to could act that way when Bone would come home," commented Peach.

"I know…look at him."

They watched him paw at the rocks a minute and then look back at them again and woofed.

"Think we're supposed to remove those rocks," said Peach.

"That's looks to be about where the X is on the map."

"Let's get 'er done, then, sweet pea," commented Peach as she pulled off her jacket and started grabbing rocks.

Stella pulled hers off too and laid it alongside Peach's on a large boulder that had fallen from the cliff in the past and joined her friend in removing the rubble.

It only took the girls a little less than ten minutes to remove the stones from the face of the nitche in the rock.

Peach shined her tac light inside and fell back on her butt. "Now, shug, that just beats all I've ever seen."

Stella knelt down, peered inside and inhaled sharply, putting the back of her hand over her mouth. "Oh...my...God!"

"Padrino said to take it out and put it down in the cellar," commented Peach as she reached inside and attempted to pick up the statue. "Good gracious. It's gonna take the both of us, girl, to get it out of there...It's heavy as grandma's fruit cake."

FLYNN RANCH
1898

Professor Cobb removed the last of the rubble around the cavity and peered inside. "My word!" He sat back on his heels and looked up at Bone, Loraine and Padrino.

"Well?" asked Bone.

Cobb took a breath. "I wasn't expecting this...Some wine or blue fresh water pearls from the *Caddo* or possibly *Atakapan*...but not pre-Columbian or even Neolithic Incan art. Please carefully remove the statue and set it outside here so I can examine it more closely."

Bone squatted down, reached inside and grasping the effigy on both sides with his massive hands, carefully lifted up enough to extract it from the nitche without bumping the top. He sat it down just outside the opening.

The professor pulled a Sherlock Holmes type magnifying glass with a four-inch black handle and held it close to the surface of the statue. He slowly passed it back and forth, taking an inordinately long time over the ruby.

"My God. I've never seen a ruby anywhere this big...it must be between six and eight thousand carats...and from what I can tell with this glass...flawless...This is impossible."

"What's impossible, Professor?" asked Padrino.

He cleared his throat. "Considering the fact that the statue itself was hand-hammered and not forged, but the ruby, however, is a perfect round cut and faceted...Well, it presents somewhat of a conundrum or even a paradox, if you will."

"What do you mean?" asked Loraine.

"Well, the gold statue is not a problem for Neolithic civilizations, but the cutting and polishing of the ruby would be impossible, not withstanding the unbelievable size of the stone...and it certainly gives all the appearance of being part of the effigy…from its inception.

BONE RANCH
2018

Peach and Stella lifted the heavy gold statuette out of its repository and set it down in front of the opening.

"Notice how warm it is?" questioned Peach.

"It's like it has been sitting in the sun…How much do you think it weighs?"

"Forty pounds, at least…Wonder if it's solid?"

"Could be, sunshine…betcha an archeologist would know, but I'm gonna say it's got a wood core. They had to have somethin' to hammer the gold nuggets on and build it up to the full statue."

"What do you think it's worth?"

"Well, darlin' I can tell you this, it's value ain't goin' to be how much gold or that doohicky three pound ruby in the center is worth…It's gonna be as an antiquity 'cause…it ain't supposed to be here."

"How so?" asked Stella.

"On account it's about 4,500 miles from the house."

"Wonder how it got here?"

"That, baby cakes, is the sixty-four dollar question."

Tyrin sniffed the statue and started running in circles and barking.

FLYNN RANCH
1898

Padrino leaned over and whispered to Bone and Loraine, "Listen, that's Tyrin barkin'. I know his sound."

Bone looked slightly confused and then a light went on in his eyes.

"Lord love a duck. The vortex is fluxin' again…Stella and Peach are at this same place in 2018, with Tyrin, at the same time we are…Wow! That's heady."

"I felt like I was tingling when we rode up, but attributed it to being a little chilly," said Loraine.

Padrino grinned. "Gives a lot of credence to Einstein's Special Theory of Relativity about the past, present, and future existing side-by-side in quantum entanglement...Spooky action at a distance."

§§§

CHAPTER SIX

BONE RANCH
2018

"Oh, my God, Peach, we're in that electromagnetic vortex thing, like when the captain got through to Bone on his cell. Quick, call Padrino, I'll call Bone."

The girls had both numbers on speed dial and hit them.

The calls rang once, twice…then three times.

"Bone," came the answer on Stella's phone.

"Padrino here…That you, Peach?" his voice came through her speaker.

"Padrino, Padrino, Padrino," she squealed. "We're here, we're here at the ridge! Oh, my God, sweetie, it's so good to hear your voice."

"I know, Peach, yours too…We heard Tyrin barkin'."

Both girls were jumping up and down and Tyrin was spinning in circles and jumping high in the air as he heard the voices.

FLYNN RANCH
1898

"Calm down, Peach," said Padrino. "Calm down."

Stella's voice came through Bone's speaker, "Bone, how's Loraine?"

"She's fine, little bit…she's right here."

"Oh, my God, oh, my God, ya'll are married! The captain and everybody else couldn't believe it."

"I know…We couldn't believe it either."

"Listen, don't know how much time we have," said Padrino as he walked out of hearing distance of the professor who was still studying the effigy with his magnifying glass and in his own world.

"Tell the captain, we don't know when we'll be back, yet. Still got some things to do."

Loraine reached for his phone. "Stella, good to talk to you, girl."

"You, too…Missus Bone." Her grin spread across her face.

"Yeah, who knew?"

"Got news for you, lady, I figured it out some time ago and knew it would hit you, sooner or later."

"What do you need us to do, Padrino?" asked Peach.

"Take beau coup pictures and measurements of the statue and some samples of the gold for analysis. We can tell where it came from, that way."

"Got you covered, Padrino…That's right up my alley."

"I know."

"Listen, Stella," said Bone as he took his phone back from Loraine. "We opened a bank account at the Cattlemen's Bank of Jacksboro, in Loraine and my names...uh, before we got hitched. We'll leave a letter of authorization, power of attorney, signed by the both of us in the back of the little alcove behind the statue under a rock for you to present at the bank." Bone nodded at Loraine.

She opened her beaded parfleche she had carried since Fiona had their buckskins made last month and took out a small notepad and pencil and jotted down a brief power of attorney for her and Bone as he continued with the conversation.

"We deposited some bounty money a few months ago and have only used a couple hundred dollars. Actually added some more bounty from a couple of cases...Been drawin' interest for 120 years. Check it out...Another nice thing about this time is guys on the wanted list usually have rewards that peace officers get if they bring them on or...."

"Okay, Bone, can do. That's a way cool deal...How much..."

The signal dropped off.

"Stella, Stella." He looked down at the screen and saw there were no bars.

BONE RANCH
2018

"Padrino?…Dang, gone." She looked over at her friend. "Bone gone, too, hon?"

Stella nodded. "That was unbelievable, girlfriend…To think we were in the same place, over 120 years separated and still talk to each other…Gave me chill bumps."

"Me, too…You know we can't tell anyone but the captain? They'll think we're bat shit crazy."

"Tell me about it…Bone and Loraine opened a bank account in Jacksboro and want us to check it out…Been drawing interest for about 120 years.

"Lordamercy, could be twenty or thirty thousand dollars in there, I'll bet…He tell you how much they deposited?"

"Uh-uh…Said he's going to leave a power of attorney for us in the alcove, though."

"This is so weird…Us havin' conversations with somebody over a hundred years ago. Kinda like havin' an albino possum for a pet."

"Say what?" asked Stella.

"You can't help but keep lookin' at it all the time an' thinkin'…that can't be real."

FLYNN RANCH
1898

Bone, Loraine and Padrino walked back over to the professor as he was getting up to his feet.

"Well, what do you think, Professor?" asked Bone.

"This is an amazing find, a truly amazing find…but it produces two major problems."

"And that would be?" questioned Bone.

"Well, first, it shouldn't be here, it should be in Peru…and second, that ruby presents a paradox, as I mentioned. I would be drummed out of the Archaeological Society if I tried to present a paper on it…I think you can understand my position."

"But, you feel it's definitely pre-Columbian or Neolithic?" asked Padrino.

"Oh, no question about that. You can still make out the stone hammer marks on the surface of the gold…Now if you were to find any supporting structures or other relics, it might make a difference…but, there's still the matter of that ruby."

"So, you have no recommendation other than if we can find some supporting data?" questioned Bone.

He nodded. "However, if you were to let me take the artifact with me back to the college, I…"

"I think not," answered Bone before Cobb could finish.

"Fact is we're going to put it back where we found it until we can get a second opinion…You can understand *our* position?"

The professor blanched a little. "Oh…uh, of course…Of course. Uh…probably the best thing."

A look of fear passed over his eyes as Padrino led him back to the carriage.

Loraine surreptitiously handed Bone the paper she had written and signed, along with the pencil. She turned around and he used her back to sign his name, and then folded the paper back up.

He stuck it in the back of the nook and placed a rock on top of it, and then replaced the statue back in its proper place.

Then Bone, Loraine and Padrino re-piled the rest of the rocks, covering the opening.

"Well, that looks pretty much as it was. Don't think anybody could find it unless they know exactly where to look," said Padrino. "North Texas covers a lot of territory.

They turned and walked toward their horses.

"Well, what say we head to town so the good professor can catch his train back to Denton...You still have the blindfold, Padrino?"

"You're surely not going to blindfold me again, are you?"

"'Fraid so. No change about needing to keep this on the quiet while we look for more artifacts or structures...Hate to shoot any trespassers, know what I mean?" said Bone, with a big grin.

"Unless they're in season," added Loraine.

Bone nodded at her. "That's very true, my dear."

Padrino whipped the red paisley bandana out of his tan canvas Carhartt coat pocket and pointed toward the buggy. "After you, Professor."

He assisted Cobb into the seat, walked around to the other side, got in, and tied the cloth around the man's eyes.

Bone and Loraine led the way back toward the front gate entrance, and then to the wagon road that headed to the northeast and Gainesville.

BONE RANCH
2018

Peach and Stella carefully wrapped the statue in a blanket they had brought in a plastic bag and laid it in the small flat bed behind the seat.

They walked back to the alcove and Stella, being the smallest, got down on her knees and shined her tac light at the back. She saw a kind of flat rock against the end and moved it off to the side. There was the paper, where it had been for a hundred and twenty years.

The girls looked at each other. Both shook their heads and said, "Wow."

Stella unfolded the page torn from a spiral pad to see both Loraine and Bone's signatures under their authorization to her and Peach to deal with the bank. They went back to the Gator.

"Jump in, Tyrin," said Stella as she climbed into the front passenger seat.

The muscular dog jumped up in the back. He sniffed the blanket wrapped around the statue and woofed when he recognized Bone and Padrino's scent and laid down beside the artifact.

"You're not going to take it to the lab, are you?"

"Oh, mercy, no, cup cake, we can take all the photos we need at the ranch. I'll get enough scrapings of gold off the bottom to run it through a whole battery of tests including my mass spectrometer…Then we'll store it in the cellar like Padrino said."

"What will that tell you?"

"Goodness gracious, honey, a whole rasher of things." She started the engine on the Gator and put it into gear. "First, I'll vaporize a sample, and then ionize it, accelerate the ions in an electric field and then deflect them by a magnetic field into a trajectory on my graph that will give me a distinctive mass spectrum…Don't you see?" Peach accelerated up a low hill and over the top. "Yeeha."

"Sorry I asked," said Stella as she grabbed the side bar handle for support.

SANTA FE DEPOT
GAINESVILLE

Bone, Loraine and Padrino escorted the professor to the southbound train, idling at the platform.

Padrino handed him five gold eagles for his

appraisal and trip. "Here you are, sir, your customary fee, as I understand it."

The dowdy academian glanced at the five twenty dollar gold coins and put them in a vest pocket. "Glad to be of service. Remember if you find anything similar, please let me know...I'll be happy to come back up."

Lawrence Clagett and Johnson Kittleson watched the professor get on the train from inside in a forward car.

"Well, the little worm got some money for his trouble," said Clagett.

Kittleson chuckled. "For us...Now, we have to find out what he saw and try to figure out where the devil they were."

Clagett nodded. "What he knows...we're gonna know, my friend."

"Board! All aboard...Denton, Fort Worth, Waco and points south...Board!" shouted the blue-clad conductor as he walked along the four passenger cars on the platform.

Professor Herman Cobb, nodded at Bone and Padrino, and then tipped his bowler to Loraine as he climbed the four steel steps up to the front platform of the third car.

The big black locomotive chugged, its four-foot tall drive wheels slipped a little as the engineer released the Johnson bar and applied power. The Gulf and Colorado train rapidly picked up speed as she left the depot behind, headed south, belching black smoke from her stack.

Loraine turned slightly to Bone. "Did you make those two con artists watching us from car number one?"

"Did…We're not through with those two I suspect."

"I figure it's their problem," said Padrino.

"Wonder if the girls found the letter?" asked Bone.

"Doesn't matter right now, they won't find it for a long time," added Loraine.

Bone shook his head and grinned. "Man, that's still hard to grasp."

"What?" asked Padrino.

"The fact that we just talked to them a bit ago and they should be just findin' the letter Loraine wrote and we signed…but they're not even born yet," replied Bone.

"They don't know that. As far as they're concerned, the letter has been there for a hundred and twenty years," said Loraine. "And it has."

"See?" Bone nodded and added, "Then what say we go by Faye's…we wouldn't get back to the ranch before midnight…Betcha she's got supper just about on…Besides, she needs to meet Padrino."

The wiry veteran grinned. "You say she's a widow lady?"

"A very attractive one, too," said Loraine.

"Uh-oh," Bone punched Padrino lightly on the shoulder.

§§§

CHAPTER SEVEN

BONE'S RANCH
2018

Peach pulled the Gator through the fourteen foot wide double doors into the big red, board and batt barn, and killed the engine.

Stella looked over at Bone's 1930 Cord under a gray, custom-fitted, lightweight, acrylic cloth car cover. "We need to take the Cord out for a drive. Not good for them to just sit up all the time."

"Sure as cornbread goes with turnip greens, buttercup. Good thought...That big inline eight engine needs to have the oil up around the cylinders regular like...but, right now, got some other work to do."

"Okay, but, hey, we could drive it down to Jacksboro to check with the bank there. I'll do a search and see if they've changed their name or anything," said Stella.

"Oh, bless your heart, sweet pea, I was fixin' to do that."

"I'll report in to the captain when we get inside and clear us going down to Jacksboro...Tell him we won't be using a city vehicle."

"That should be almost good as the Balm of Giliad."

"What does that mean?" asked Stella.

"Balm of Giliad was a rare perfume used medicinally in Bible times made from poplar tree buds...It's kinda come to mean a universal cure...in figurative speech."

"How do you know all that stuff?"

"Shug, it's like I told you, I got more degrees than Carter's got little liver pills…'Sides, I do surely love to read an' readin' to me is like gravy comin' with biscuits…'cause you always learn somethin'."

Stella just shook her head, blinked twice, and grinned.

The girls got out and lifted the statue from the rear deck and, with one on each side, carried it up the steps and into the house followed closely by Tyrin. They walked down the long twelve foot wide dog run to the kitchen and set it on the breakfast table.

The room still smelled of chocolate chip cookies they had baked last night.

"I'll get my kit to take the samples, you start takin' pictures an' measurements," said Peach as she turned around and went back outside to the car.

"Can do." Stella took out her Galaxy S9 phone and started snapping shots from every angle, distance, and different zooms.

Peach walked back in with her kit and set it on the table next to the statue. "Tilt that little puppy over, hon, so I can scrape a few curls of gold from the bottom."

Stella leaned it over while Peach grabbed a small tool, somewhat related to a narrow potato peeler and took a couple of swipes across the underside of the soft metal base. She put the thin shavings in a couple of glass vials and stoppered them.

"Now, have to take this to my lab in town to vaporize it and run it through my mass spectrometer."

"Can you x-ray it to see if it's hollow or has a wood core?" asked Stella.

"Gold is impervious to x-rays, much as lead, babe...only more so. The only way I know of to find that out would be to calibrate the total mass density and cubic weight of the statue with a water test."

"Water test?"

"Uh-huh...kinda like doin' a body fat ratio test in a water vat. We know that gold has a mass density of 19.3 grams per cubic centimeter where lead is 11.4, for example...See?"

"No...and never mind...that stuff gives me a headache...I have no desire to know what my body fat ratio is anyway, so as Bone would say...'Don't care...just don't care'," she said in her best imitation of the big man.

BONE'S GOLD

"But, it's like I said before, it's my understandin' that back in the Neolithic time, before they could smelt metal, they carved a core out of wood and hammered the almost pure raw gold nuggets on it until it was built up to three or four inches...More than a tad thicker'n gold platin', honey."

"That's why it's as heavy as it is, then?"

"Now you're cookin' with gas, doll...It probably has a small wood core...not that it really matters much. That ruby is worth more than the gold, but the antiquities value is worth a whole bunch more than the both of them put together."

GULF & COLORADO TRAIN

Lawrence Clagett and Johnson Kittleson stepped through the front door of the third passenger car and moved down the aisleway to near the center. They sat down in the forward-facing double seat in front of Professor Cobb, in the rear facing one.

"Well, fancy seeing you here, Professor. How was your trip?" asked Kittleson.

The little man jumped when he looked up from his newspaper at the men as they took seats across from him. Sweat began to bead almost immediately on his upper lip as his face noticeably blanched.

"Uh, gentlemen…Uh, well, uh, not too good."

"Meaning?" asked Clagett as he frowned and squinted at him.

"I saw their find all right, but I was blindfolded and have no idea where we were."

"Oh, come now, Professor, you can sit there and say you don't have any idea where you were?…What do you take us for?" said Kittleson.

"Well, uh, I mean I feel confident we were either in southwestern Cooke County or maybe southeastern Montague County."

"Uh-huh…so what was their find? You do know that, don't you?" asked Clagett.

"Uh, yes, gentlemen…It was a gold Neolithic statue with a rather large ruby in the center."

"Gold?" both said simultaneously, sotto voce.

Kittleson glanced around to make sure no one in the sparsely occupied car was listening. "How big?"

Cobb took a breath. "Around eighteen inches tall by eight wide…approximately forty pounds."

"Forty pounds of gold?" repeated Kittleson.

The professor pinched his lips and nodded.

"How about the ruby?" asked Clagett.

Cobb lowered his head and leaned toward the two men. "Between six and eight thousand carats."

"What? What did you say?" hissed Kittleson gruffly, also leaning forward.

"Six to eight thousand carats...that's between two and a half to three and a half pounds," he said slowly.

"A three pound ruby?" said Clagett in wonder.

Cobb nodded. "There abouts...But, I couldn't certify the find."

"Not that we care, but why not?" asked Kittleson.

"Considering the age of the statue...the people that created it did not have the ability or wherewithal to cut and polish the gem...not to speak of the faceting...It's impossible. I would have to see more finds or other supportive data."

"But, you saw it?" demanded Clagett.

"I did. It presents quite a paradox`. It shouldn't be there, it can't exist...but there it was."

The two grifters looked at each other.

"Tell you what you're going to do, Professor, you're going to write a detailed description and sketches of what you were able to see once they took your blindfold off...I mean everything, the statue, every hill, every tree, every rock...Do you understand?" said Kittleson.

"What were their names? The people that took you there," asked Clagett.

"Uh, the elder gentleman who wrote the letter was named Jethro Pereira, but preferred to be called Padrino and the other two were deputy sheriffs, a Mister and Missus Bone...I believe her first name was Loraine."

"Yes, we met them, they surprised us back on the trail and killed a friend of ours...We owe 'em," said Clagett.

"What county were they deputies of?" asked Kittleson.

"Uh, didn't think to ask."

"Figures," mumbled Clagett.

FAYE SKEANS BOARDING HOUSE

"Faye, this is my Padrino," said Bone as they stepped into the parlor of her ornate Queen Ann style, three-story, red brick, boarding house.

"Padrino...Faye Skeans."

He took her hand and kissed the back of her fingers. "It's a true pleasure, Madam. I've heard so much about you, but their description was woefully short of your breathtaking beauty and did you no justice at all." Padrino flashed his amber gold eyes at her as he raised back up.

A very flustered Faye Skeans blushed deeply, fanned her face with her left hand and stammered. "Why…Padrino. You take my breath away with your manners and…"

"We done good, Pard," Bone interrupted her and nudged Loraine with his shoulder.

"I can tell," she answered back.

Faye's blue-gray eyes also twinkled. "As Angie McGann would say, 'I think you're gifted with a bit of the blarney'," she said with a big grin. "But, I love it…You just keep it up, you hear?"

"I shall do my best, my dear Faye." He tilted his head at her.

She hooked her arm through his and walked the three into the parlor with a crackling fire roaring in the fireplace.

"By the way, what's your real name?…I know Padrino is what you go by. What did your mama name you?"

He grinned. "Jethro Barthelomew Pereira, it's Portuguese."

"Ooh, I like the name Jethro…Why don't ya'll have a seat, supper's almost ready."

"Oh, we don't want to impose, Faye," said Bone.

She looked askance at him. "Bone, don't pull that on me, I know you too well…Ya'll've been staying here for almost three months…I'll have your rooms ready in a jiffy, too…Loraine, will you help me in the kitchen for a moment?"

"Of course, Faye."

The two women exited through the dining room, and then the two-way door into the kitchen.

"Dang, Padrino, you're smoother than banana puddin'. Didn't know you were so handy with the ladies."

He got a wry grin on his face. "There's a lot of things you don't know about me, Bone."

They heard heavy steps on the porch and turned to see Texas Ranger Bodie Hickman come in the front door. He hung his hat and gunbelt on the hat tree in the foyer.

The big rawboned redhead entered the parlor. "Well, looky here, looky here…Ya'll lost? Thought

I left you over to the Wilsons," he said to Bone and Padrino standing in front of the fire.

"Did, Ranger, but you won't believe what we fell into now," answered Bone.

"Well, let's have it," Bodie replied.

§§§

CHAPTER EIGHT

BONE'S RANCH
2018

"How does that look?" asked Stella.

Peach looked at the wooden case Stella had spent the last two hours making from a couple of old apple crates she found in the barn. "I do declare, girl, but you missed your callin'. I thought that it was gonna be a bit tacky when you started, but, uh-uh, not so, sugarboo."

"Thank you, m'lady." Stella did a slight curtsy. "Thought we'd put the statue in there first, and then pack some coastal hay from the tow sack I brought in around it...Should to be as good as that popcorn foam stuff."

"If common sense was lard, most people couldn't grease a cake pan, but you done good, girl. Padrino ought to be tickled...Be safe as a baby in it's crib."

"It is pretty good, isn't it?" Stella said, stepped back, looking at it again and smiling.

"Well, let's put this little soldier in there, pad him up good and tote the whole thing down to the cellar," commented Peach.

They set the statue inside, packed almost a flake of the hay around it and nailed the lid on the box.

"Now, won't nobody know what's in it, in case they were to go down in the cellar and this is with those other boxes and the put-by veggies and pickled peaches Padrino and Bone have stored down there."

"Then let's go into the office. I saw some plastic sleeves in the desk we can put the letter in and you can Google the bank and see if it still has the same name," said Peach.

"Wonder if that letter was in the back of that alcove when we first took the statue out?"

Peach looked at her friend and cocked her head. "Had to be. They put it there one hundred and twenty years ago."

"But, we just talked to them and they hadn't done it yet," argued Stella.

"Sweet pea, even Einstein couldn't figure it out. That's why he called it 'spooky action'."

"Oh, boy," Stella said as she sat down at Padrino's computer, opened Chrome and punched in the name of the bank in the Google search.

"Well, that didn't take long."

"What's that?" asked Peach as she looked over Stella's shoulder.

"It's now Jacksboro State Bank."

SKEANS BOARDING HOUSE

"...and that's the way it went, Bodie," said Bone.

The ranger pushed back from the table after they finished the story and Faye's pot roast.

"My goodness, I'd love to meet those ladies of ya'lls…'Specially that one from Valdosta, Georgia. Momma said we had some relatives named Presley, that lived in Valdosta…What'd you say her Christian name was?" asked Annabel.

"I think she told me it was Betty Mae, but she'd been called Peach since she was little," said Loraine.

"Speakin' of names…Did you get 'em for those two yahoos you caught followin' you?" asked Bodie.

"Nope, messed up there," answered Bone.

"Well, not really. We can go by Doc Wellman's office. I would imagine he got their names when they brought the body in…He's the county coroner. The undertaker won't accept the body without a death certificate from the coroner," commented Bodie.

"And if not, they bought tickets today to Denton at the Santa Fe Depot on the Gulf and Colorado. The agent would have their names also," added Loraine.

"And here's desert," said Faye as she came in the room from the kitchen through the swinging door. "My special steamin' hot peach an' apple, floating crust, cobbler."

The enticing aroma of the cinnamon laced sweet confection permeated the room almost instantly.

"Oh, yum," said Bone as he caught a whiff.

Faye set the large cast iron Dutch oven on a hot pad near the corner of the table.

"All right, start passin' your desert saucers down this way. I believe there's enough of my fresh butter in the bowl there, so help yourself, I have more in the ice box." She filled the first saucer and passed it on around the opposite direction.

Everyone at the table was salivating at the thought of dipping into Faye's scrumptious after dinner reward.

"This smells almost too good to eat, my dear Faye," offered Padrino.

"Go on with you, kind sir. There you go again." Faye smiled and gave him a little extra to go along with her wink.

"I didn't finish, m'lady…I was going to add, that I didn't have the resistance to just smell and look at it," Padrino replied with his own wink. He took a bite and closed his eyes as he savored the flavors. "Oh my stars. This is wonderful, my dear Faye.

There's a hint of something else besides the cinnamon…Is that nutmeg, by any chance?"

Faye blushed again and continued dishing out the cobbler. "Just a pinch." She grinned. "You have quite the discerning palate, Mister Pereira."

He nodded and smiled at her as he slipped the fork back into the flaky crust.

Bodie swallowed his first bite. "Oh, golly gee, Faye this is awesome."

"Only one helpin' this time, mister. I can't let your pants out anymore," said his blond wife, Annabel. "Eat it slow, honey bunch."

Bodie ducked his head a little. "Yes, dear." He also remembered the advice Cletus Wilson had given he and Bone after they took care of the Rudabaugh gang. *The secret to a long and happy marriage, gentlemen, is two simple words…Yes, dear'.*

"This is absolutely decadent, Faye," said Loraine after taking her first bite.

"What does that mean?" asked Bodie.

"Scrumptious," answered Padrino.

"Why did she just say that?"

"Thought I did, Bodie." Loraine grinned and then continued, "Now if we can get those fellows names, any chance the Ranger head office in Austin will have any information on them?"

"Most likely...The captain's office assistant keeps a running file on wrong doers in the state from reports sent in by field rangers, sheriffs, marshals and the like."

"That's one good thing about our time...in law enforcement."

"What's that, Bone?" asked Bodie, and then he took another bite.

"All arrest and investigating data, pictures, fingerprints and the like is available from a central source by that computer that I've mentioned to you before. We can log in and get a complete history and background of a suspect in a matter of minutes."

"Wow, that would be so much help. It can sometimes take us months to collect all that kind of information, even with the advent of that new telephoney thing of Mister Bell's."

"We didn't start getting that kind of available information until the 1970s or '80s, wasn't it, Pard?" commented Bone.

Loraine nodded and dabbed her mouth with her napkin. "They established the NCIC, the National

Crime Information Center, in 1967 through the FBI. That's the Federal Bureau of Investigation—the national police force. It will be founded a few years from now in 1908."

"Now that will be neat," said Bodie. "But, for now, gotta do with what we got."

"*Zip- a- dee-doo-dah, zip-a-dee-ay, My oh my what a wonderful day…*"

"What is that, Bone?" asked Faye.

"Oh, it's just a song from one of those play-acting motion picture things we've mentioned called *Song of the South*…Neat story. About the post Civil War…Wish we had a copy and a way to show it to you."

"That not withstanding, we'll probably be seeing those two guys again and the more information we have on them, the better…They'll most likely bring along some friends," added Loraine.

"I have no doubt the professor reported what he saw to those two. I think they've got something on him and are using him as a bird dog," said Bone.

"What does 'bird dog' mean?" asked Annabel.

"Means they're using him to smell out deals that they can profit off of, my love," answered Bodie. "I agree, Bone, sounds like they're blackmailing the poor jaybird to funnel information to them…especially on valuable artifacts an' such…Probably not the first time."

"When he tells them about that gold statue and the ruby, I think we can count on some major trouble," said Loraine.

"That was the main reason we blindfolded the professor," offered Padrino. "We'll still be overrun by treasure hunters up here. The rumor of gold treasure will spread like wildfire."

"That particular spot down in the southeast corner of Cooke County will be like a needle in a haystack…Cobb won't know if he was in Cooke, Wise or Montague County. Not to mention gates and fences," said Bone.

"What if they find it?" asked Faye.

"Well, just the fact that Peach and Stella found it in 2018…where we left it, is pretty good proof that they didn't, my dear," replied Padrino.

"True, but what about the rest of it?" questioned Bone.

"Rest of it?" asked Bodie.

Padrino nodded. "That statue was just the tip of the iceberg…In my vision, there was a large amount of gold and other valuable items that sect of the

Nasca, Bone and I are descended from, brought with them up to this part of Texas in about 100 BC...I'm confident the larger portion of the treasure is in the Brazos valley in Palo Pinto County."

"Oh, boy," commented Bodie.

JACKSBORO STATE BANK
JACKSBORO, TEXAS
2018

"Right this way, officers," said Mervin Prather, the head teller as he knocked on a door with the gold lettered name in the center—Henry Blubaugh - President.

"Enter," came the voice from inside the office.

"Mister Blubaugh, these police officers would like to talk with you."

Henry got a puzzled expression on his face and then a frown. "Uh, yes, of course. Come right in ladies...Prather bring us some coffee, please."

"Black," said Stella.

"Mine too, honey," added Peach.

He nodded and closed the door behind him.

"Have a seat, have a seat...Now, is this an official visit?"

"Mister Blubaugh, I'm Inspector Stella Johnson and this is Forensics Technician Peach Presley. We're police officers from Gainesville in Cooke County." She flipped open her leather case and showed her gold badge.

"Oh...well how may I be of service?" he asked.

Peach opened her case and removed the letter from Bone and Loraine in a plastic sleeve and laid it in front of the president.

"As you can see, Mister Blubaugh, this is a power of attorney from a couple of depositors of this bank when it was known as the Cattlemen's Bank of Jacksboro."

He perused the document. "My goodness, this is from 1898...Darrell Ulysses Bone and Loraine Maria Rodriguez. I'm not familiar with the names."

"I'm sure...but if you'll check the account numbers there, I'm sure you'll have records of their deposits."

He turned to his computer and clicked in the numbers, scrolled the screen and suddenly stopped. His face blanched. The president turned to Stella and Peach.

"Yes, I've found the numbers, but, that was over a hundred and twenty years ago. I'm sure any deposits have been claimed by heirs by now."

"Sweetheart...bless your heart. Thought you might say something like that. As you can see from the document...For all intents and purposes...we are the heirs," said Peach.

Stella cocked an eyebrow and leaned forward with a slight smile. "Mister Brubaugh, just a tip for the wise...I wouldn't want to be sitting where you are...If Peach here ever says, 'Sweetheart' and 'bless your heart', in one sentence...shit's about to get serious."

§§§

CHAPTER NINE

DENTON, TEXAS

An exhausted Professor Herman Cobb walked down the dark, winter killed, tree shrouded, street toward the small home he and his wife occupied only four blocks from the depot.

It was a partly cloudy, moonless night making negotiating the short trip more difficult than it should be.

Cobb thought he heard a noise behind him. He stopped and wheeled around.

"Who's there?"

The sound stopped.

Dog, he thought, turned and continued his way, only two blocks to go.

He heard it again—stopped once more and tried to look back in the darkness. "Who is it?"

The professor turned back toward his direction to home and picked up his pace. One block to go.

He could see the light of the candle his wife always left in a front window of their house in the distance when he was going to be late and began to relax a little.

Cobb felt a tremendous impact to his back and he pitched forward on his face in the hard packed dirt of the street. The pain was intense. He tried to roll over, but was pinned to the ground by a massive weight.

Then there was something around his neck. The professor reached up with his hands, but it was too late. The piano wire loop, known as a *garrote*, was already tightening. He couldn't breathe. Panic set in and he thrashed as hard as he could, but to no avail. His vision dimmed from lack of oxygen as his tongue protruded from his mouth. The night became black as pitch—and then—he was still.

The weight disappeared from his back as his assassin got to his feet, rummaged through Cobb's pockets and removed the five gold double eagles, and then vanished into the night.

ODYSSEUS SALOON
DENTON, TEXAS

"Here's your two eagles," said Clagett as he handed Kittleson the coins. "I'm keeping two." He set a single twenty dollar gold piece on the table and chuckled. "We'll use this one for drinks, till it's gone."

The other man nodded. "That'll do.

They motioned for the bartender.

Charles Martin, the balding, overweight, proprietor walked over. "What'll it be boys?"

"Bourbon and branch, for me," said Kittleson.

"Sour mash, neat, you don't mind." Clagett pushed the double eagle toward the bartender.

"Back in a minute," said Charles.

"You know, Lawrence, I been thinkin'."

"Uh-oh, here we go," Clagett replied.

"No, listen…That statue can't be the only thing out there." Kittleson arched his brow at the other man. "Got to be a lot more where that came from."

They quit talking when Charles brought their drinks. "Want your change now, or do I wait a bit?"

"Be a good idea to wait a bit, Martin. We're not done, yet."

"Whatever you say." The bartender spun on his heel and walked away.

"You were sayin', Johnson?"

"Why try to bust our butts tryin' to find that one statue when it stands to reason the old codger, man-mountain and his wife are goin' to look for the rest…If they don't already know where it is."

"Good point. But, they were pretty slick spottin' us somehow," said Clagett after he took a sip.

"I know this half-Comanch, named John Horse, we can hire for damn little to shadow 'em till they go to where the rest is."

"Knows his stuff, I take it?"

101

"You don't see him unless he wants you to."

The two con-men clicked their glasses and drank to the new approach.

SKEANS BOARDING HOUSE

"Well, I don't think it's any question the bad guys are goin' to be after you like a duck on a June bug," said Bodie.

"Already noticed that with those three we confronted following us yesterday. Apparently that professor shot his mouth off before he came and that probably means double when he got back home after seein' the statue," replied Bone.

Bodie stepped over to the fireplace to warm his backside against the chill of the winter cold outside. "I don't have anythin' pressin', right now...how's about I go with ya'll if you're goin' down in the Brazos to look around? Spent more'n a couple of days in that valley chasin' outlaws...Used a lot by renegade Injuns and bad guys on the scout."

"Probably a good idea, Ranger. The sheriff and Fiona are going to be stickin' close to Jacksboro, now that she's showin'," said Padrino.

"Show Bodie a picture of Tony," commented Loraine.

"Tony?" asked Bone.

"That's what I'm calling that statue…after Tony Stark. He's the Iron Man in the comics and movies in our time. Has that red thing on his chest?"

"I have no idea what you're talkin' about, Loraine," replied Bodie.

"Iron Man is a fictional character that's kind of a flying robot with a man inside, Tony Stark. On his chest is this round red thing called an arc reactor…that's his power source…Looks like that big ruby on the statue's chest. So, I call him Tony," she said.

"Hey, works for me, Pard." He reached over and they bumped fists.

Bone got out his Galaxy phone, opened it to his gallery, scrolled over to the statue and showed it to Bodie."

He grinned. "That thing's slicker'n a greased baby's butt. Wish I had one…Be great for Ranger work."

"Does come in handy," replied Bone.

He showed Bodie how to zoom in or out on the picture and handed him the phone.

"Wow, is that ruby as big as it looks?" he asked.

"About three pounds or so," replied Loraine.

"Whoo-lolly, dang…double dang…That alone will bring 'em outta the woodpile," Bodie said, shaking his head.

He looked at Padrino. "So, you think there's more?"

"No question, Bodie. Saw it in my vision."

"Lucy said his visions are really memories," said Bone.

"Don't really wanna know. All that gives me a headache. You're here, that stuff is out there…Let's go find it. The bad guys are gonna be comin'…That's all I need to know," commented Bodie.

"We'll head that way in the morning," said Bone.

JACKSBORO STATE BANK
JACKSBORO, TEXAS

Mervin Prather opened the door to President Henry Blubaugh's office and walked in with a tray carrying three cups of coffee. He set the tray on a coffee table and handed a cup and saucer each to Stella and Peach, and then to the president. He set a small silver creamer and a matching bowl of sugar on the table, along with three spoons.

"Will there be anything else, Mister Blubaugh?"

"I think not, Mervin, thank you. Close the door on your way out."

"Yes, sir." He turned to Stella and Peach and nodded. "Ladies."

After the door was closed, Blubaugh looked at the girls. "Now, how do I know that document is real?"

Stella set her cup down on the table. "Mister Blubaugh...Miss Presely and I are both officers of the court. We testify quite regularly...me as a crime investigator and Peach as a forensics expert. If she says it's legitimate and authentic, you can take that to the bank...pardon the pun."

"Sweetheart, before you throw a conniption, I don't really think you want to get in that dog fight...You'll lose, trust me," added Peach with a smile. "You're not from around here are you?"

"No, I'm from New York."

Peach nodded. "Uh-huh."

"Now, what's the current balance of the account?" asked Stella, her antique gold eyes burned a hole in Blubaugh's hazel ones.

He keyed in some numbers and then glanced over at the screen—the color drained from his pudgy face as he broke out into a cold sweat. He pulled on his collar like it was too tight, and then said, "Uh…uh…the original deposit was $5,500 in 1898, another $6,250 added over the next three months, $500 was withdrawn…It was converted to an interest bearing trust in 1908…Now with interest averaging four percent over 120 years, compounded quarterly, comes to…$1,334,786.91," he mumbled.

"How much?" asked Stella.

Blubaugh took a breath. "One million, three hundred thirty-four thousand, seven hundred eighty-six dollars and ninety-one cents."

Peach and Stella exchanged glances without a change of expression.

"Best leave it sit until we tell you different, Mister Blubaugh. We'll need to find out where we can put it, but it's good here for now," commented Stella.

"We would, however, like a notarized document from this bank…and you as President, stating that amount is in the account, with a *complete* activity ledger, and that Stella Diane Johnson and Betty Mae Presley are the legal joint executrixes, of said account...That satisfactory, sugah?" asked Peach.

"Uh, yes, ma'am..."

"It's Miss, Mister Blubaugh," corrected Peach.

Stella and Peach got to their feet.

"Thank you for your time, Mister Blubaugh, we'll be in touch," said Stella. "Please express that document, certified, to the Gainesville Police Department within twenty-four hours."

Blubaugh got to his feet and started to walk them to the door. Stella held up her hand and shook her head that it wasn't necessary.

They headed out the door and to Bone's Cord parked in the front of the bank and got in. Stella started the big Lycoming straight eight, eighty-eight year old engine that purred like a kitten.

She pulled the first front wheel drive automobile in America out into Archer Street and headed east. They turned north on Bowie Street which became Highway 59 that would take them to FM 1810 and eventually through several other Farm Market roads back to the ranch near Rosston.

As they rolled down 59, Peach asked Stella with a deadpanned expression, "Did you notice Brubaugh when he got up?"

Stella nodded her head.

"My grandma always said, 'Never trust a man whose ass is wider than his shoulders'."

"True."

They stopped just outside of town, both calmly removed their sunglasses, got out of the Cord Cabriolet convertible—Stella walked around to the shoulder where Peach was already standing.

They looked at one another for a moment, and then went into a hug, jumping up and down and screaming for almost forty-five seconds. Then they broke apart.

"Did you hear what he said?" squealed Stella.

"Verbatim, honeychile…One million, three hundred thirty-four thousand, seven hundred eighty-six dollars and ninety-one cents!"

§§§

CHAPTER TEN

SKEANS BOARDING HOUSE

"I've packed you a lunch along with your trail supplies. Now ya'll be careful...especially you, Jethro, you hear?" said Faye.

"Wouldn't have it any other way, sweet lady," he replied.

"Thanks for the supplies and the lunch, Faye, Pap Clark brought a pack horse over yesterday evenin' with panniers...Don't know how long we'll be out, so we'll probably pick up some more supplies in Joplin," said Bodie.

Annabel gave Bodie a big hug and kiss. "Now, you come back safe, sweetie pie, you understand. I don't want to see any more holes in you...ever again."

He hugged her back. "Yessum, that's the plan."

"Like they said on one of our play-acting shows that was on the television, 'Let's head 'em up an' move 'em out'," said Bone.

"That television thing sounds facinatin', Bone," commented Faye.

"It can be...and can be quite addictive up to the point that it's often referred to as the 'idiot box'," added Loraine. "But, it occasionally has it's place...Never replace a good book, in my opinion, though."

"Especially in the '50s and '60s when the majority of the entertainment shows were westerns...and now we're living it," said Padrino with a big grin. "A lifelong dream."

Faye gave Padrino a rather long hug, also, and then followed everyone to the door. She and Annabel waved goodbye from the big, wide, wraparound porch as the four untied their horses at the street in front of the house and mounted up.

Bodie led the pack horse, dallied off to his saddle horn, as they trotted north on Dixon Street to California Street, west, which would take them to the west side of town.

No one noticed the half-breed Comanche, John Horse lying on the ground under a large, low-growing wisteria on the opposite side of the street, a half-block to the south. He had lain under the shrub for over two hours with the patience known only to the Indian.

Padrino purchased a fifteen-hand claybank gelding from Pap Clark—they were getting acquainted.

"How's he ride, Padrino?"

"Pretty smooth, Bone…Has a good slope to his shoulder, that's why I picked him out of the bunch Pap had in that trap…Like his eyes, too."

"How so?" asked Loraine.

"Wide set…usually a good sign of intelligence. Narrow-eyed horses tend to be mean and ornery."

"You mean like Bone?"

"Hey, hey, hey, woman. I'm just about the nicest feller I know."

"You've just led a sheltered life, Bone," said Padrino.

Loraine giggled. "Finally, somebody to help me keep the big galoot in line."

"That's right, gang up on the big guy."

"If you insist," said Padrino.

"How come you let Faye call you Jethro? You always said you hated that name."

"Never had anyone like Faye to use it before...I like it." Padrino glanced over at Bone out of the corner of his eyes with his Sam Elliott look. "But, not you."

"Goin' to be like this the whole way?"

"Not likely, Ranger...Your time's comin'," replied Bone, grinning. "When you least expect it."

BONE RANCH
2018

"Did you notice how warm that statue was?" asked Stella.

"I did, sweet pea, especially the ruby part...even after bein' in the house overnight."

"Wonder why?"

"We'd have to ask Lucy...an' that's not goin' to happen...or maybe Padrino will know."

"If anybody does, he will, he'll poop green bricks when he finds out how much Bone and Loraine have in the bank over in Jacksboro."

"Ya think?" Peach paused in thought for a moment. "You know, our phones worked with them when we were both around the statue...Don't suppose..."

"Dang, girl! You're smart even when you aren't trying to be...That's it!"

A light came on in Peach's clear blue eyes. "Well la-de-frickin'-da...I see where you're goin', baby cakes. Lucy said these rubies are made by their people an' are used to collect energy...solar and cosmic rays, for their various devices...Like the power generator here in the house an' her bracelet." She grinned and nodded. "The ruby on the statue was partially opening the portal vortex enough for us to get through on our cells."

The girls looked at each other for a moment, and then simultaneously whipped out their cell phones.

"I got Bone," said Peach.

"I'll do Padrino's," replied Stella as they both hit their speed dial.

COOKE COUNTY
1898

"Stella! How'd ya'll get through again?" asked Padrino as he picked up on the second ring after digging it out of his jacket pocket—then he heard Bone's *William Tell Overture* ring tone.

"We figured it out, Padrino."

"What?"

"How we're able to get through...It's the crystals, especially the big one on the statue which is right under our feet," said Stella.

"But, we aren't near...No, wait. My *moldivite* crystal in my pocket and Bone has the bracelet Lucy gave him...Think you're right."

"Hey, Peach, what's shakin'?"

"Bone, Bone, Bone, Bone, ya'll won't believe...It's like havin' pecan pie for breakfast with Blue Bell Country Vanilla ice cream."

"What, Peach? Slow down. Make sense, girl."

"Ya'll's account in Jacksboro."

"Yeah, what about it?"

"One million, three hundred thirty-four thousand, seven hundred eighty-six dollars and ninety-one cents!"

"What?"

"It has one million, three hundred thirty-four thousand…"

"Heard you the first time."

"Then why…"

"Just wanted to hear it again…Good golly Miss Molly."

"What do you want us to do with it?"

Bone thought for a second. "Okay, take it…"

They were cut off, and then back on.

BONE'S RANCH
2018

"Where?" she asked.

"Take it to First State in Gainesville, open a trust…Peach?"

"I'm here. What about estate taxes?"

"Good question. Thanks to our wonderful President Trump, there are no estate taxes below $5.6 million now."

"Ooh, ooh, ooh, right. We'll...Bone? Bone?"

The connection was broken.

COOKE COUNTY
1898

"I think we may be able to get through almost anytime ya'll are close to the statue and I have my crystal in my pocket." Padrino noticed Bone had lost contact. "It's probably stronger than Bone's little one on the bracelet."

"Peach is nodding and mouthing she got some instructions from Bone...We'll...Padrino? You there?...Huh...guess not."

BONE'S RANCH
2018

Stella put her phone back in her pocket. "What'd you get from Bone, Peach?"

She giggled again. "The big hunk sounded gabberflasted when I told him how much money was in their account."

"I guess so…What did he say to do with it?" Stella asked.

"Said to bring it to the First State an' open a trust…That there were no taxes 'cause of what our president got passed, bless his heart."

"I'd feel a lot better with it being in Gainesville anyway. Wonder what kind of interest we can get?"

"Probably not as much as the past hundred years or so…Specially not on an open account. A trust will be a whole bunches better."

"Right, I really don't trust jug butt over in Jacksboro any further than I could throw him."

"Well, honey, he is from New York City, not countin' that his ass is two ax handles wide."

COOKE COUNTY
1898

John Horse studied the road, following the tracks of the five horses—one set was distinctly large.

"Big man, got big horse." He almost smiled.

The tracker could tell that they were at least five miles ahead of them. "They no lose John Horse."

The half-breed had asked the ticket agent at the Santa Fe depot, when he rolled into town, if he knew where a big deputy sheriff, named Bone, lived. He had a message for him.

"Shore, everbody knows 'bout man-mountain Bone. Him an' his purdy wife live over to Skeans Boardin' House on Dixon, 'long with Texas Ranger Bodie Hickman an' his wife...Cain't miss it," said the young agent. "Tell 'em Marvin Clearwater said hydie."

"Uhh, me do," replied the surly Indian.

"All white men fools," he muttered softly after he walked out the door.

§§§

CHAPTER ELEVEN

COOKE COUNTY
1898

"There's a million three in our account in 2018?" said Loraine.

"Plus thirty-four thousand, seven hundred eighty-six dollars and ninety-one cents, Pard."

"I know, I know…Now what are we going to do with that kind of money when we get back?" she asked.

"If we get back…That's a big assumption, hon," Bone replied. "And don't forget about all that gold and those diamonds we still have out at the ranch…even after the girls bought the place next door for us."

"I think we can go back anytime we want, now that we know about how the crystals affect the electromagnetic vortex," said Padrino.

"What if we jump in that thing and it sends us to a different time…other than home?" asked Loraine.

"Ooh, good question, Pard. We don't have any idea if it actually works or not," replied Bone.

"Ya'll confuse the hell out of me," said Bodie. "First, it was you couldn't go back until the next blue moon in June, 'cordin' to *Anompoli Lawa*, then Padrino comes, an' ya'll start talkin' with your friends in 2018 through those phone things, an' then find out you're richer'n old Ben Gump an' now you don't know if you're goin' back atall…I don't get it."

Bone chuckled. "You put it that way, Bodie, I see your point."

"Well, we still have some things to do in this time period yet," commented Padrino. "This is the only time frame we have current access to where we can try to find the rest of our people's legacy down in the Brazos valley since it's all underwater after 1931."

"There was a reason we came here in the first place," said Bone. "We've saved my great grandmother's life, but according to *Anompoli Lawa*...we always did. So, we're just fulfilling destiny. Then we saved a future president's life...don't know what effect that had, but again, it was still part of the past..."

"And we actually belong in 2018, so if we go into that vortex, we should return there," said Loraine.

"Do we?" asked Padrino. "I don't think we'll really know until we do it...meanwhile, let's enjoy our time here...I'm lovin' it."

"Not that Faye Skeans has anything to do with it," suggested Bone with a big grin.

"I think it's cute," said Loraine.

"Ya'll are goin' to drive me crazy," commented Bodie.

Bone rubbed the back of his neck. "I think we're being followed…again."

"Gut?" asked Padrino.

Bone nodded. "Always trust your gut…I just sense a darkness back behind us, it's pretty dim, but still there."

"Gets any stronger…let me know," offered Bodie.

"Maybe I ought to drop back and check it out," said Bone.

"Don't think so…Not yet. Hell, we don't even know where we're goin'. Got some miles to cover first," replied Bodie.

GAINESVILLE PD

"So, that was pretty much the way that went, Cap'n. Supposed to get that doc by express today, but I got an itchy feelin' down my back," reported Stella.

"Have you checked to see if he's been handled before?" he asked.

Stella and Peach exchanged glances.

"No, and that's a good point, sir."

"I know. That's why I'm sitting on this side of the desk...That's an awful lot of money that's been sitting there for a long time...Temptation, temptation...and you don't think he knew until he pulled it up?"

"Judgin' from his expression when he saw it on the screen...No," answered Stella.

St. John grinned and shook his head. "Hell, leave it to Bone to fall in a septic tank and come out smelling' like a rose."

"I'll bet if Blubaugh's been handled, I swan if the temptation isn't goin' to be too much for him?...Kinda like an egg-suckin' dog."

"How do you mean, Peach?" asked Stella.

"Can't break 'em of it. Once they get a taste of easy pickin's...they'll always go back."

"Well, I suggest you ladies go find out...now." The captain slipped his glasses on, looked down at the paperwork on his desk for a moment, and then back up. "Today, girls, sometime today."

"Yessir, yessir," they said together, shot to their feet and headed out the door.

They walked into the detective's office down the hall from the chief's. Stella sat down at her desk and Peach at Bone's.

Both started pulling up data bases, Stella keyed her password and logged into NCIC while Peach opened the New York State court records.

"Well, well, what have we here?" Stella leaned into her monitor and scrolled through some entries.

"Find somethin'?" asked Peach.

"Something," replied Stella. "One Henry Blubaugh...Arrested on two counts of embezzlement from Hudson Insurance...acquitted. Key witness failed to show."

"Found it...Jury trial. Four hundred-fifty thousand missing from two equity accounts. Head of the accountin' department..." She grinned. "Uh-huh...Disappeared. Missing persons report..." Peach looked up. "Never cleared."

"Surprise, surprise...Ah-ha, got another. Arrested for felony fraud on a loan application to a National bank."

"Ooh, that's a no-no. Get any time?" asked Peach.

"You won't believe."

"Try me."

"Initiating loan officer from the complainant bank...was a no-show at the trial." Stella looked over at Peach. "Disappeared."

"How the hell did he get the job of President of a bank?" asked Peach.

"Out of state and it was a state bank not a National, plus five'll get you ten, they bought his phony resume and nobody checked up on him."

"Either that or he had a picture of one of the majority stock holders doin' somethin' really weird with a dog in the back yard."

"Oh, yuk, Peach."

"It happens, buttercup, it happens...There's two things in this world that have a really ugly underbelly...big business an' politics." Peach grinned. "An' like Mammy Yokum would say, 'Ah has spoken'."

"Print what you have, I'll do the same and we'll take it back down the hall to the Chief."

They both hit print and waited a few seconds as the machines spat out the reports.

Stella grabbed them up, stapled them together and put them in a manilla folder.

"Here we go," said Peach as they headed out the door and back down to Captain St. John's office.

Stella laid the folder on his desk and they sat down in the straight back wooden chairs across the desk, facing the Chief.

St. John put on his reading glasses and perused the documents in the folder. When he finished, he looked up at Stella, and then Peach. "Get that express letter yet?"

The girls exchanged glances.

"Uh…no," replied Stella.

"What the hell are you doing sitting there?"

Their eyes got big as saucers, they looked at one another again, and then got to their feet.

"Laterbye," Stella said, mimicking Bone's habitual expression on departing.

"And watch your backs," St. John said as they left.

They turned in unison and scooted out the door.

"I'll call Chief Haney," he yelled as they disappeared down the hall.

"Get your gear, Peach, and meet me in the parking lot at the black wrapper…We're outta here…What did he say?"

"Somethin' 'bout our hineys."

Stella frowned. "Whatever." She got her purse and what she thought she might need and headed to the parking lot across the street from the station.

Five minutes later, they passed the Gainesville city limits sign on Hwy 51, which would take them southwest to Decatur and from there, they would get on 380 to Jacksboro.

The GPS in the unit said it was seventy-six miles and one hour and sixteen minutes travel time.

Forty-eight minutes later, the black sedan passed the Jacksboro city limits sign on Hwy 380 which became Main Street. They turned left on Archer and pulled up in front of the Jacksboro State Bank and stopped.

"Ready, girl?" asked Stella.

"Honey chile, I was born ready," she said as she opened her door and got out.

They strode through the big plate glass doors into the lobby and straight to Blubaugh's office. The head teller, Mervin Prather, moved toward them.

"Just a minute, officers, you can't just walk in there."

"Watch me, sweet cheeks." Stella burst through the walnut door with the gold-lettered name on the outside: *Henry Blubaugh - President*.

The somewhat corpulent man standing behind his desk looked up as he was cramming papers in a black leather briefcase. "What's the meaning of this?…You can't…"

"We just did, chubby," said Stella.

He sneered at them. "They send two helpless girls into my office?"

"Sweetheart, the only time I might be helpless is when my fingernail polish is wet…But, I can still pull a trigger if I have to," retorted Peach.

Blubaugh reached toward an open drawer in his desk with his right hand.

Stella whipped out her Glock 19 from under her jacket and aimed the 9mm weapon between his eyes in a two-handed, modified, Weaver stance. "You better have a lollypop in your hand, lard ass, when you pull it out of that drawer."

Her antique gold eyes took on a chatoyant gleam as a wry grin crossed her face. "I'll show you helpless."

"We'll take it from here, Inspector," came a voice from behind her.

§§§

CHAPTER TWELVE

ODYSSEUS SALOON

"How often is that half-redhide supposed to check in?" asked Lawrence Clagett as he took a sip of his sour mash.

"Every town he comes to," answered Johnson Kittleson as he looked at his empty glass.

"What if they don't go through any towns?"

Johnson motioned to the bartender, Charlie, and held up two fingers. "Told 'im we wanted a telegram ever two days…one way or another."

"Think we can trust 'im?"

Kittleson glared at his partner as Charlie set two fresh drinks on the table and walked back to the bar. "No, that's why I sent Ace McQueen an' his little brother Gunn to join up with him."

"Those crazy gunslicks?"

Kittleson nodded. "Might be crazy…but do what they're told."

"Either know what the old man an' the others are lookin' for?"

Johnson picked up his glass and took a long drink, and then set it back down. "Not hardly…Gold and treasure can tend to warp a man's thinkin'. All they know is they're gettin' fifty apiece…They should be able to catch up with Horse 'bout the time they get to Era or Slidell."

"How so?"

"Horse'll be trackin'…they know what direction he was headin' when he left Gainesville…Can travel a lots faster."

"I'm thinkin' we may need mor'n those three. They had that Texas Ranger join up with them, you know...An' you remember the size of that pistol man-mountain was carryin', don't you?" asked Clagett.

"Oh, I do...I do, indeed. Looked like a damn cannon. Blew a hole in Parker you could stick your fist through...That's why I got hold of the McQueens...None of 'em are bullet proof."

COOKE COUNTY

"What say we swing by and see Lucy an' them? Not far out of the way. I 'spect we can be there in about two hours or less," said Bodie.

"You just know it'll be suppertime when we get there," replied Loraine.

"When you're right, you're right, Pard," added Bone with a big grin.

"Not a bad idea, Bodie. Bone and her together may get a better feel of who's behind us," commented Padrino.

The four entered the tall cedar post entry of the Wilson Ranch and trotted the mile and a half to the house.

Lucy was standing at the gate in the white picket fence surrounding the front yard of the rambling shiplap-sided ranch house. Garin sat patiently beside her.

Loraine waved as they came into sight. The diminutive pixie-haired alien, masquerading as an abandoned child adopted by the Wilsons, waved back.

She opened the gate as they rode up to the hitching rails just outside the fence and dismounted. Garin spun around several times and butted the big man's leg.

"I know, you knew we were coming," said Bone as he leaned over and scratched the pit bull's ears.

Lucy grinned and nodded as Mary Lou came out on the porch.

"It's a good thing she did, I was able to increase the amount of stew I had in the pot. Cletus shot a buck yesterday…Got plenty now and the cornbread is almost ready."

"See," said Loraine as she looked at Bodie.

"Oh, wow, love venison stew," exclaimed Padrino.

"Have two buttermilk pies coolin' on the window sill, too."

"I have died an' gone to heaven," commented Bodie as his eyes brightened.

"Take care of your horses first." She slapped her flour sack dish towel on her thigh. "Cletus is out in the barn, he'll help you pull your tack an' feed 'em...Then ya'll wash up." Mary Lou turned and went back in through the forest green gingerbread screen door on the front of the house.

John Horse, Ace and Gunn McQueen looked at the tracks leading into the entry of the Wilson Ranch.

"What they goin' in there for?" questioned Gunn as he sucked on a stick of butterscotch hard candy.

"Why doesn't little white man ride up to house an' ask."

The blond-headed wiry gunhawk looked over at Horse. "Why don't the half-breed take a flyin' leap up my ass."

"Uhh, John Horse might do that...but, little white eyes never see comin'," he said without glancing at the younger McQueen.

"Awright, that's enough. It's purtnear suppertime. They probably know these people an' are goin' in for a feed...I say let's us go set up a camp back at that creek we crossed thirty minutes ago. Far enough away, we kin build us a small fire an' boil up some Arbuckles."

"Uhh, good." Horse nodded. "Plenty trees between creek an' house down way." He pointed the direction the road led.

JACKSBORO STATE BANK
2018

Stella turned her head slightly at the two Jacksboro plainclothes cops behind her and Peach in the doorway, both had their handguns drawn. She returned her focus to Blubaugh, still frozen in position with his hand in the drawer.

"How did you guys know to be here?" she asked, over her shoulder.

"Your chief called our chief," said the larger of the two plain clothed detectives, Bill Dunlap, with a smile. "He filled him in with all the details…Good work."

Detective Dunlap and Detective Nichols stepped inside the office and separated to each side of the girls, giving them a good angle of fire on the bank president.

"Now, Mister Blubaugh, like the lady said, if you don't have a lollypop in your hand, I'd be real slow in removing it from the drawer," said Dunlap.

All four of the officers maintained their weapons on Blubaugh.

"Now! Do it now!" he added.

Blubaugh's complexion took on a pasty pallor as his fat cheeks quivered. There was an audible thump and he slowly lifted his hand out of the drawer—empty.

"Art, check it out," said Dunlap.

The other Jacksboro cop holstered his S&W M&P40, stepped forward and around the side of the desk next to Blubaugh. He peeked in the drawer, pulled a blue latex glove from his suit coat pocket and, without putting it on, reached inside, picked up a stainless steel Colt Python .357 magnum revolver with a three inch barrel and showed it to the others with a grin.

"Ohh, that's nasty. Good instincts, Inspector," said Dunlap.

"I was taught by the best," she replied. "Darrell Bone."

"Oh, right, been here giving us a blood-spatter class…Big sonofabitch knows his stuff."

"You wouldn't believe, sweetie." Peach moved forward with a gallon freezer zip-lock bag and held it open for Art. He dropped the pistol inside and she zipped it shut.

Officer Nichols then grabbed Blubaugh's right hand, none too gently, whipped it behind the fat man, then pulled his left to the back, also, and snapped his cuffs on. He spun the defrocked bank president around, shoved him against the wall, and patted him down.

"He's clean," he said. "You have the right to remain silent. Anything you say can and will be used against you in a court of law. You have the right to an attorney."

"You hayseeds got nothin' on me."

"Yeah, that's what they all say…We just like to practice saying the Miranda Law."

Peach donned a set of surgical gloves, her's were purple, snapped the briefcase closed and did a quick scan of the desk.

"Thanks, Miss Presley, our tech people are on the way, but I'm sure they would appreciate someone of your rep to work with them."

"Honey, this may take a while, this guy is crooked as a dog's hind leg. Not the first time he's been handled...Got a good computer person?"

"Yeah, that's what we heard, and yeah, we do."

Stella returned her Glock to its holster when Blubaugh was cuffed and yelled over her shoulder. "Prather! Get in here."

The slight-built middle-aged mousy teller, who had been standing just outside, immediately entered, "Yes, Ma'am?"

"I want a complete printout of that account in question numb nuts here looked up yesterday. Let's see if any of it has been transferred and if so...where and when. There's three possibilities and the first two don't count...and you're probably going to have to schedule a complete audit from the time this guy came on board to now."

"Yes, Ma'am, right away." He spun on his heels and headed to the accounting department.

Two Jacksboro uniformed police appeared at the doorway.

"Need anything, Bill?" one of them asked.

Dunlap turned. "Hey, Patrick, yeah, take Mister Blubaugh here and book him...threatening a peace officer for starters, we'll have more later, I'm going to say. Park him in an interrogation room till we get there."

"You got it."

The two officers entered the office, took Blubaugh by the arm from Detective Nichols and escorted him to the front door and outside to their black and white squad car.

The bank's employees and customers all watched the president being taken from the bank in handcuffs. Most were pointing and whispering to one another.

The first Jacksboro detective turned to Stella and Peach. "We didn't get a chance to introduce ourselves. I'm Detective Bill Dunlap and this is my partner, Detective Art Nichols."

She grinned and stuck out her hand. "I'm Inspector Stella Johnson, Gainesville PD and this is our forensics specialist, Peach Presley...Happy to meet ya'll."

"Yessum, we knew your names. Got 'em from our Chief Haney, an' he got 'em from…"

Stella turned to Peach. "I thought you said Captain St. John said something about our hineys."

She shrugged. "Oh, hush your mouth, buttercup, it was close enough for government work."

Dunlap and Nichols looked at each other, raised their eyebrows and grinned.

"Peach speaks a foreign language…Deep south," said Stella.

"I don't talk with an accent, sweet pea, ya'll just listen with one."

The two men grinned again.

"What say we take you ladies to lunch while we're waiting for good ol' Mervin to pull together that printout for us…Like bar-b-que?"

Stella and Peach exchanged glances.

"Thought you'd never ask," they said together.

§§§

CHAPTER THIRTEEN

WILSON RANCH
1898

"They're evil, Bone," said Lucy.

"Thought as much. I could feel 'em, but just a little."

"How many are there?" asked Loraine.

"Right now, three...but they're thinking about bringing more later."

"Why later?" asked Padrino.

"After you find the treasure," said Lucy.

Bone got to his feet and paced across the porch.

Padrino leaned over to Lucy and whispered, "He has a habit of pacing when he's pondering something."

Lucy whispered back, "I know." She grinned.

"All right, let's follow the ranger's suggestion and let them alone...for now. However, I may slip upon their camp some nights just to listen in."

"And play a prank or two?" commented Loraine.

He got his enigmatic grin. "It can happen."

"What if they spot you?" asked Bodie.

He laughed. "Not in this lifetime, sunshine."

Bone touched two of the runic type symbols on his bracelet. The air around him shimmered briefly and he disappeared.

Bodie shot to his feet. "What the..." He looked around the porch almost in a panic. "Oh...oh, that invisibility stuff you pulled up in the Kiamichi Mountains on the Roosevelt trip."

The air shimmered again and Bone reappeared.

"The same, thanks to Lucy. She had this made for me in our time after she was rescued…Comes in handy on occasion…starting with when we took on the team from that oil company that came out one night to burn this house down in 2014."

"I take it they didn't succeed?" asked Bodie.

Bone, Padrino and Loraine all grinned.

"Not hardly," offered Padrino.

"They brought out explosives, fire-bombs and some heavy duty automatic weapons," said Loraine. "You should have seen the look on their faces when Bone stuck that big .50 cal out of the field and shot one of the bad guys that was going to throw a fire-bomb. The damn muzzle flash lit up the whole area." She glanced over at her husband. "Bone materialized right in front of the leader. The guy says, 'Where the hell did you come from?'"

Bone picked up the story, "Told him I had the *Asgard* beam me down." He chuckled.

"What's the *Asgard*?" asked Mary Lou.

"There was one of those TV shows we've mentioned in our time named *Stargate SG-1*, which was a very close depiction of Lucy's people, the *Anunnaki*, only they named them the *Asgard*…If they only knew," commented Padrino, shaking his head. "They traveled all over the galaxy through portals called Star Gates, in addition to their ships."

"What makes you think they didn't, Padrino?" asked Lucy with a smile.

"Ah…kind of like your people talking to Gene Roddenberry and the *Star Trek* people you will tell me about that we've discussed already?"

Lucy, grinned and nodded. "We have communicated with many of your brightest and most innovative minds throughout the last two millennia…Aristotle, Pythagoras, Newton, Da Vinci and Tesla, to just name a few…I've mentioned we've contacted Tesla before…He's actually the latest."

"Don't start any of that, I haven't figured out the first stuff Lucy told us about with the space battle that caused her to crash," said Cletus.

Bone paused a moment and frowned.

"What is it, hon?" asked Loraine.

"Was just wondering what would have happened if I hadn't stuck my .50 cal outside the field before I fired it?"

Lucy grinned. "It wouldn't have been pleasant, Bone…Believe me."

He nodded. "What I thought."

"I don't get it," said Bodie.

"Just think of getting inside a steel barrel and somebody put the lid on and you shoot your .45 inside there," commented Loraine.

"But, I...Oh!...Oh, damn, see what you mean."

"Wonder how the girls made out at the bank?" asked Loraine.

"Guess we'll have to wait till they go back out to the ranch to be near the statue and call us," answered Padrino.

"That's still so weird, that we can be at the same place, but in different times...and talk to one another," said Loraine.

"Einstein said he thought spacetime was sometimes a matter of perception," offered Padrino.

"Who? How do you mean?" inquired Bodie.

"He was one of our great scientists of the twentieth century...Have you ever noticed that when you are in a moment of intense activity that time seems to slow down?" asked Bone.

"I don't understand," said Bodie.

"I remember playing football in college and on occasion during the heat of action, so to speak, that everything seems to slow down. I mean that everyone around me would look like they were moving in slow motion…"

"Like in a gunfight?" interrupted Bodie.

"Exactly," added Loraine.

"I gotta go get some more coffee," said Cletus as he got to his feet. "I don't have any idea what ya'll are talkin' 'bout." He opened the screen door, shaking his head.

"I think that's pretty close," commented Lucy. "We know that the faster we go in our ships, the slower time passes. Which is why we don't age when traveling at many times the speed of light through a fold in space."

"A worm hole," added Padrino.

"Yes…It's over a hundred light years from our planet Tyrin, to Tellus, but we come and go in a matter of minutes," Lucy added.

"You arrive at the same time you leave…realistically."

"That's pretty much it, Padrino," she answered. "But, our scientists feel that we could actually be arriving before we left, in real time, since we are technically traveling much faster than light…And that the present is absolute…there is only one."

"What if the present is actually the past?" questioned Bone. "We wouldn't know, because our perception is that where ever we are…is the present."

"Dang! Wish ya'll would quit talkin' 'bout it. Whenever I think I'm beginnin' to understand all this…one of you adds somethin' else."

"That is often how we figure things out, Bodie," offered Lucy.

JACKSBORO STATE BANK
2018

"I do have to say, guys, those were some the best ribs I've ever had, thank you!" said Stella as they walked back into the bank.

"Toldya," replied Detective Dunlap with a twinkle in his light brown eyes.

"Can't believe Peach bought three bottles of their homemade sauce," added Detective Nichols.

"I though I'd had good bar-b-que sauce before back home, but Hayley's was even better'n my grandpa's," she replied. "His was a sweet type, but

Hayley's has a bit of a bite to it…some type of chili pepper with no sugar…Good, uh-huh."

"Course ya'll could always come back over for some more…or something," said Dunlap.

Peach grinned. "Or somethin'."

Mervin Prather approached the group with a stack of printouts in his hand that he handed to Stella. "He did try to have a half-million transferred to an account in the Caymans this morning. Apparently he wasn't aware of the size and status of the account in question until you had him look it up…"

"Did it go through?" asked Peach.

He looked at the tall brunette and shook his head. "No, Miss, it was still in the system. It normally takes twenty-four hours for an international transfer to be processed…Especially one of that size."

"My grandma was right," Peach said.

"About what?" asked Detective Nichols.

"'Bout never trustin' a man whose ass is wider than his shoulders…Specially a yankee." She got a big grin across her face. "There are two kinds of people in the world, honey…Southerners an' those who wished they were."

"I'll buy that, Miss Peach...Plus, have to keep your grandma's platitude in mind. Might come in handy in our line of work."

"You can call me just plain Peach...Art...Or just call me." She held up her little finger and thumb to her ear.

The large former professional football player with close-cropped brown hair, blushed, and then grinned. "That'll work."

Stella leaned toward Bill and grinned. "Southern girls are known to speak their mind."

"And where would you be from, Inspector?" he asked.

"Texas."

"What about Texas girls?"

She grinned and winked at the tall detective. "Us too."

Stella turned to the head teller. "Mister Prather, please have the entire trust account transferred to the First State Bank in Gainesville. Peach and I will sign off on it and give you the name of the officer to direct it to."

He nodded. "I'll get the paperwork prepared, Miss. Give me about thirty minutes. I'll have the accounts department on it."

"Take your time," she replied as she turned and looked at Detective Dunlap. "I'm sure we can find something to occupy our time.

BLACK CREEK
1898

John Horse, Ace and Gunn McQueen had set up a camp in a secluded area several hundred yards south of the road on the creek.

Gunn was building a hat-sized fire beside some large rocks adjacent to the clear limestone bottomed creek.

"When's that coffee gonna be ready, little brother?" asked Ace.

"Keep yer pants on, be ready in a short. You could slice up some fatback, if you were of a mind whilst I get the beans on."

"I can do that," he replied as he opened their poke sack and took out the waxed butcher-paper wrapped side of fatback.

Ace laid the slab on a flat rock, pulled his razor-sharp Green River knife from the sheath on his belt and sliced some thick cuts of the smoked pork side meat. He laid them in the small hot skillet sitting on another flat rock next to the fire pit where they immediately began to sizzle.

Gunn turned to Horse. "Hey, breed, why don't we move up a little closer to 'em when they git back on the trail?"

"Uhh, no need. John Horse no lose tracks...Big man know we follow...not care...For now."

"What makes you say that?"

"John Horse just know."

§§§

CHAPTER FOURTEEN

WILSON RANCH
1898

The sun peeked over the eastern horizon, throwing red and gold arrows across the sky to the west. The heavy early morning frost on the winter-killed blue-stem and gamma prairie grasses took on the look of a light coating of scintillating diamond dust as the sun's rays glinted from it.

Bodie threw a final half-hitch around the panniers on the pack horse tied up next to his and the other's out in front of the Wilson house.

"All right, folks, let's mount up," said Bone as he stuck his foot in Hildebrandt's left stirrup and swung easily into the saddle.

Padrino, Loraine and Bodie followed suit.

They waved goodbye to Lucy, Mary Lou and Cletus, standing on the porch.

Lucy jumped down and ran up to the white picket fence, followed by Garin. "Bone, don't look, but, we're being watched…Treeline west of the road."

He nodded and got a wry smile. "Figured."

"Well, makes things interesting," said Loraine.

"Keeps it from getting boring," added Padrino.

The foursome turned and trotted toward the rutted ranch road over a mile from the house that led southwest in the direction of the Brazos.

John Horse squatted down under a female Juniper loaded with its winter crop of purple berries, and watched the group almost a half-mile away mount up.

He faded into the brush behind the tree, backward like a crawdad, until he was far enough to turn and run silently through the thick woods toward the camp by the creek.

"How far back do you think they're trailing?" asked Loraine.

"Four or five miles, I suspect. Those two grifters that hired them undoubtedly recanted how that gunhawk with them met his demise a few days ago," said Bone.

"They probably think we won't notice them that far back," added Padrino.

"Figure we'll camp next to Waggoner Branch near Paradise tonight," said Bodie.

"Paradise? That's where Mason and Fiona found Lucy, wasn't it?" asked Bone.

"And where he got shot in the back when he was mistaken for his outlaw twin brother, Dixon," said the ranger. "I was with 'im."

"Mason got shot?" exclaimed Loraine.

"Yep…Actually, he died…But, Lucy and Fiona brought him back," replied Bodie.

"Like they did Bone, when he took that bullet in the chest for Fiona," * said Loraine.

"Mason had a twin?" asked Padrino.

"Uh-huh…Dixon. He was kidnapped by Comanches when they was 'bout two and raised up by one of Quana Parker's wives till the army brought them all in to Fort Sill, when he was fifteen."

Bodie reached in his vest pocket and pulled out a plug of Brown's Mule Chewing Tobacco, bit a chunk off and put it back in his pocket, and then continued, "They didn't know who he was, see, just that he was a kidnapped white boy…Put him with a drunkard who beat him all the time…till Dixon got tired of it an' killed him, ran off an' took up the outlaw trail…Me, Fiona, Brushy Bill, an' Mason had to track him an' his gang down when folks started thinkin' he was his outlaw brother…Mason was forced to kill him," replied Bodie.

"He had to kill his own brother?…Oh, my," commented Loraine.

"Dixon wadn't about to go back an' git hung, so he drew on Mason…but, never pulled the trigger."

"Who won?" asked Padrino.

Bodie looked over at Bone, and then Padrino. "Dixon."

"So, he wanted his own brother to kill him," stated Loraine.

Bodie nodded.

"Wow, that's a hell of a story…twin brothers, one a lawman, the other an outlaw…Bet somebody writes a book about that one day." **

"Probably right, Bone," commented Padrino. "There are a lot of western novels written in our time that have a lot more truth to them than many people might realize."

Bone grinned. "You think?"

STEELDUST by Ken Farmer - 2018
**FLYNN* by Ken Farmer - 2017

BONE'S RANCH
2018

Peach and Stella walked into the kitchen in their pajamas and looked over at the automatic coffee maker almost full of the morning brew.

"So much better to get up in the morning and the coffee's already made," said Stella as she got two mugs out of the cabinet.

Tyrin, pranced about, his entire body wiggling.

"Well, you sweet thing, you're hungry, aren't you?" asked Peach.

Stella glanced at his stainless steel bowls. "He's probably hungry and thirsty, since both are empty."

"Uh-oh...Shame on us, we didn't check before we went to bed," said Peach.

"Serves us right for getting in at midnight."

"But, we got to do some two-steppin' to Robert Joe Vandygriff...He is so good...Cute too."

Stella grinned. "Him or Bill and Art?"

Peach glanced over at her as she put a teaspoon of raw sugar in her cup. "All of 'em, honey bun, all of 'em."

"Speaking of honey buns, how about we put a couple in the microwave, with a dollop of butter on top, an' nuke 'em?"

"Umm...sounds good," said Peach as she filled Tyrin's water bowl, and then opened the big plastic forty pound tub of Blue Buffalo Wilderness Chicken Grain Free dry dog food and put two large scoops in the other.

All the time she was getting his water and food together, Tyrin was bouncing up and down on his front feet with the front of his upper lip curled back in an obvious smile.

"Sweet baby was hungry, wasn't he," said Peach as she set his food bowl down next to his water.

The blond and white pit bull butted her leg and answered with a rumbling type of growl, "Woo, woo, woo."

"You don't need to fuss at us."

He stuck his face down into the bowl and grabbed a mouthful of his favorite dry food.

Stella pulled her phone out of a side pocket on her jammy bottoms and held it up. "Shall we?"

"OMG, Buttercup, you knew what I was thinkin'." Peach got her phone out. "Got Bone."

"Good for me." Stella hit her speed dial for Padrino.

WISE COUNTY, TEXAS
1898

The four were moving down the ranch road about three miles south of Decatur at a road trot when both Bone and Padrino's phones ring tones sounded.

"What the sam...Oh, those telephony things," said a startled Bodie.

"Girls must be at the ranch and up," said Padrino as he answered his phone. "Hey, Stella."

"Yo, Peach," said Bone. "What's shakin'?" He put his Galaxy on speaker.

"We got it done, Bone," said Peach.

"Uh...Good. Got what done?"

"All ya'lls money transferred to Gainesville...and it was a good thing, sweetie."

"Because?"

Stella joined in, "Seems that the president of the bank in Jacksboro was crooked as the Brazos and when he found out how much was in the account, he tried to transfer a half mil offshore."

"He was a real lard-ass, too...The captain suggested we run a NCIC search an' sure 'nuff...embezzlement an' fraud for starters, along with disappearin' witnesses," added Peach. "We cut him off at the pass by gettin' back over there yesterday before the transfer could go through..." said Peach.

"He's now occupying a suite in the Jack County steel motel...curtesy of Detectives Dunlap and Nichols," interrupted Stella. "Captain St. John had called over and gave their chief a heads-up we were coming."

"Heard of 'em," commented Bone. "Good cops."

"Cute too," said Peach. "Good ol' bucket butt tried to pull a .357 magnum on us."

"What happened?" jumped in Loraine.

"Stella beat him to the draw." Peach giggled. "We heard a loud thud as he dropped his Python back in the drawer when he looked down the barrel of Stella's Glock aimed between his eyes."

"Then the cavalry showed up and took over," added Stella.

"Ya'll done good, kids. Wish you were here."

"What's goin' on there?" asked Peach.

"Oh, we're just headed down to where Possum Kingdom Lake is in our time, but is a bunch of deep canyons where the Brazos cuts through that big limestone ridge is there in this time period...That's where we think the rest of the Nasca treasure like that statue is...an' we got some bad guys on our tail to see if we find it," said Padrino.

"Just the three of you?" asked Stella.

"No, got Texas Ranger Bodie Hickman with us," said Bone.

There were squeals coming through Bone and Padrino's speakers.

"The Texas Ranger Bodie Hickman?" the girls screamed together.

"Yeah, say hi to Stella Johnson and Peach Presley, Ranger...Cops from our time," Bone said as he stuck his phone toward Bodie.

"Uh...kin ya'll hear me?" he shouted.

There were squeals again. "Yes, yes," they said together.

Peach added, "But, you don't have to shout, honey, we're not deaf."

"Dang, you sound just like my wife, Annabel."

"Aw, really?...How sweet. Wherebouts she from?"

"Mobile, Alabama...Born an' raised."

"Bless her heart. Tell her I said hidydo," said Peach. "I got some kinfolks from Mobile."

"Where are you from?" asked Bodie.

"Valdosta, Georgia...That's why they call me Peach...Christian name is Betty Mae."

"I'll tell her when we get back…She won't believe I was talkin' with two ladies over a hunderd years from now…Ain't sure I believe it."

"It's way cool," said Stella.

"Naw, it's actually purty warm here, today…For December," replied Bodie.

Bone, Loraine and Padrino all exchanged looks and grins.

"We'll explain later, Bodie," said Loraine.

§§§

CHAPTER FIFTEEN

WISE COUNTY, TEXAS
1898

"Looky there, they ain't even tryin' to cover their tracks...Hell, even I could track 'em," said Gunn McQueen pointing down at the hoof prints of the five horses. "What makes you think they know we're trailin' 'em, breed?"

"Little white eyes already say."

"What?"

"They no try to hide track. They no care if bein' followed."

"Then I don't understand why we're follerin' 'em way back here like this."

"Little white eyes no understand many things."

"You know, breed, I'm gittin' damn tired of you callin' me little white eyes."

"Then grow some an' become Injun or 'breed',"
commented John Horse dourly. "Meby just call you *pin-dah-lickyoee*."

"What in hell is *pin-dah-lickyoee*?"

"Apache for 'white eyes'."

"Damn you, half-breed…"

"Awright, you two, that's enough. We may have to git into a set-to, with that bunch, 'fore this is over…No need in wranglin' with one another…Gunn, I suggest you jest keep yer trap shut," said Ace.

"Kiss my rusty, big brother…I ain't sceered of that half-redhide." He looked over at John Horse.

The tracker only glanced at him out of the corner of his eye and almost smiled.

"Where you think they're headed, Horse?" asked Ace.

"Go as bird fly to Brazos canyons." He pointed with his hand like a hatchet.

"Gunn, you go into Paradise an' send that telegram to the boss…"

"Why me?"

"'Cause I said so, that's why."

The younger brother reined his horse to the left muttering, "Coulda sent the damn Injun."

"Coulda, but he cain't write, you can…An' stay out of the saloon. Send the telegram an' git yer ass back here."

"Yeah, yeah," he said as he rode off.

WAGGONER BRANCH

The group searched along the south bank of the creek for almost a mile before they found a suitable campsite as the sun was setting. It was overcast and darkness came quickly as usual this time of year.

The winter-grass covered glade was apparently once a north loop of the waterway left after the branch meandered back to the south several hundred years in the past.

There were plenty of large rocks that could be used to bank the fire against, not to mention a plethora of good, dry, deadfall and driftwood from past floods plus good grazing for the stock.

"I'll hobble the horses over there." He pointed. "After I water 'em and strip the tack...if ya'll will build the fire and get some coffee on," said Bodie.

"I'll do the cooking...tried both Bone's and Padrino's," commented Loraine as she dropped her sougan where she intended to sleep.

Bone and Padrino exchanged glances.

"Guess that leaves us to build the fire and gather wood," commented Bone.

"You get the wood, I'll do the pit and start the fire. I see a big downed cottonwood over yonder I can get phylum from inside the bark to make some punk with," added Padrino.

Thirty minutes later, their tack was all placed in the camp in their respective sleeping spots...Bone and Loraine's were side-by-side...and the fire was going. She had some beans, fatback and hot-water cornbread on cooking.

"Coffee's ready," said Loraine.

"Bout time, thought I was going to have to take over," commented Bone.

"In your dreams, doofus…Had to let it boil twice…which you don't do," countered Loraine.

"I just figure everybody can strain the grounds through their teeth, hon."

"You can do that, Bone, you use a railroad spike for a toothpick anyway."

"Ouch, you're gettin' better, Pard."

"Self-protection."

"Easy to tell ya'll are married," said Bodie.

"Oh, this is just a continuation of how we acted before we found out we were in love…It's a habit," replied Loraine.

"It's how we show our love," said Bone as he pecked Loraine on the cheek.

"Boy, don't want to be around when ya'll get into an argument," commented Bodie.

"Confucius say, 'In marriage arguments…much like in surgery…the knife must be used with care.'," Bone added as he bowed with his hands together in front of him.

"That won't save you, Bone," replied Loraine.

"They just move the furniture back," said Padrino, with a big smile under his full white mustache.

Bodie grinned and shook his head. "Maybe Annabel an' I oughta try that...she can start an argument in an empty house. Plus she can slice you ten different ways and you won't know it for two days."

Loraine giggled. "Sounds like Peach. That girl can say more with the cut of her eyes than a week of speeches by a room full of Senators in Washington...and she has the ability to go from sweet southern belle to country crazy in about three seconds."

"What's for supper, baby cakes?" asked Bone as he brought another armload of deadfall and dropped it near the fire pit.

"Ya'll notice how nice he gets when it's about food?...Look in the skillets, big boy."

Bone held up his hand and put his fingers to his lips. He cocked his head, and then faded into the moonless, overcast darkness beyond the light of the fire into the woods on the south side.

"Helloo, the camp," came a cry from the darkness on the north side of the camp, opposite from where Bone disappeared.

"Come on in, but keep your hands where we can see 'em," replied Bodie.

A rough-looking individual wearing a battered and dirty gray Stetson, walked into the edge of the firelight, leading a scrawny bay horse with a thin blaze down his face. "Smelled yer coffee."

"Leave your horse back yonder and come on in, if you got a cup," said Bodie.

"Shore thang…'preciate it." The apparent cowboy tied his mount to a branch, pulled a tin cup from his saddlebags and stepped back into camp. "Smells good."

"Help yourself," said Loraine.

"Name's Easy, Easy Pickins."

"Real name?" asked Padrino.

"Naw, got it a few years back playin' cards in a cow camp…'nuff said. Where ya'll headin'?" He squatted down, grabbed the pot with one of his gloves from his belt and filled his cup.

"Just passin' through," said Bodie. "You?"

"Same…Lookin' fer work."

"Cowhand?" asked Padrino.

Easy nodded and took a sip. "'Mong other things."

"Like?" inquired Loraine.

"Whatever might be profitable."

"That a fact?"

"Uh-huh."

"Travelin' alone?" asked Bodie.

"Sometimes."

"Like now?" inquired Padrino.

He took another sip and got to his feet. "Not so's you'd notice." Easy pitched the rest of his coffee into the fire causing a cloud of steam to boil up into the cold night air drawing everyone's attention to it.

"Stand and deliver!" came a voice from the top of a barrel-sized boulder to the right of where Easy entered camp.

Bodie, Padrino and Loraine looked in the direction of the voice to see a similarly dressed cowboy standing atop the rock with a Winchester held at his hip, pointed in the direction of Bodie.

"Is this how you repay a welcome to our camp?" asked Loraine.

"Gotta do what we gotta do," answered Easy.

"Shuck your hardware," said a voice as the owner of it stepped out from behind Easy's horse with his Colt in his hand.

"Takes three of you to rob a camp?" asked Padrino.

"Naw, four," came another voice from near the creek as he too stepped into the firelight also with a Colt.

"Five," said one more coming from around the boulder.

"You boys are makin' a big mistake," commented Bodie.

"And why would that be?...We got you outnumbered," said the man on top of the boulder.

"One, I'm a Texas Ranger, an' this lady here is a Deputy Sheriff of Jack County."

"And I'm just a mean and ornery old man who hasn't killed anyone today...yet," said Padrino.

Bodie transferred the graniteware coffee cup to his left hand. "And two, you really don't think we're dumb enough to just let you yahoos stroll into our camp, do you?...An' just so you know...you're about to piss me off." He squared off with the man on the huge boulder.

"Haw...That supposed to skeer us?" said Easy.

"No, but another Deputy Sheriff out in the dark has one of you in his sights, right now...Wonder which one it is?" added Bodie with a big grin.

The five tobymen exchanged nervous glances.

Finally the man on top of the boulder spoke, "We think you're blowin' smoke, Ranger...Ain't nobody else out there."

"Thought I said to shuck yer hardware?" said the man who had stepped out from behind the horse.

"I don't think so," replied Loraine.

A deep voice rang from the darkness behind Loraine. "Mirror, mirror on the wall...who is goin' to be the first to fall?"

"Gawdamighty!" said the man on the rock as he brought his rifle to his shoulder.

He never got a chance to pull the trigger on Bodie as his chest exploded in a cloud of pink mist and his body was blown backward off the rock at the simultaneous sound of a tremendous explosion. Both his feet flipped up over his head as he disappeared into the black night behind the boulder, limp as a rag doll—dead when he hit the ground.

The darkness at the back of camp was momentarily lit up like it was daylight from the muzzle flash of Bone's huge .50 cal—then it went dark again.

The other brigands, after being stunned for a second, turned to fire, but Bodie, Padrino and Loraine quickly drew their sidearms and the night exploded in muzzle flashes again, this time with screams, and the roar of .45 caliber semiautomatic fire.

"I give, I give!" yelled the man who had stepped out from behind the boulder, as he curled up on the ground in a fetal position with his hands covering his face.

He was covered in blood and gore from the man who had been on top of the rock.

"Oh, God, please, please, don't shoot no more…please," he blubbered through his hands.

Bone stepped into the ring of light, holstering his Smith & Wesson and shaking his head. "Time and effort will take care of ignorance…but stupid is forever."

§§§

CHAPTER SIXTEEN

WAGGONER BRANCH

"Think we should carry the bodies and the prisoner into Paradise now?" said Loraine as she walked back into camp from washing the dinner things down at the creek.

"'Spect so, Loraine, shore don't want 'em stacked up like cordwood there overnight. Be drawin' varmints…not to say anything about gettin' ripe," said Bodie. "Plus, not in the mood to baby sit the survivor."

He turned to the prisoner sitting on the ground, his hands behind his back shackled with Bone's cuffs. "What's your name, Slick?"

The young man looked up. "How'd you know?"

"How'd I know what?"

"My name."

"I just asked you, Slick."

"That's right." He nodded.

Bodie shook his head and looked at Loraine. "Well, this is gettin' nowhere."

"Shades of *'Who's on First'*," mumbled Bone.

"Think he means his name is Slick, Bodie," said Padrino.

Bodie turned back to the highway man. "That right, Slick?"

"Uh-huh."

"Why didn't you say so?"

"Didn't have to, you did."

"Oh, boy…Where are ya'll's horses?"

"Back yonder."

"Here we go again."

"On your feet, Slick, show us," said Bone.

"Ya'll take them in, I'll stay here and watch the camp...No fair getting rooms at a hotel or anything," commented Padrino.

Bodie chuckled. "We won't. The only hotel in Paradise is where Mason died an' came back to life...the Rhine Hotel. Belongs to Constable Muller's wife...They're German immigrants." He shook his head. "He doesn't carry a gun...Mason asked him why and he said, 'I don't need ze firearm. I am ze Constable.'"

"Surely you jest," commented Bone.

"Fun you not...He's a case."

"I'll help ya'll load the bodies before they get too stiff," said Padrino.

"Lead the way to the rest of your horses, Slick," commented Bone as he pointed toward Easy's horse still tethered to the limb.

"Got a last name?" asked Bodie.

"Uh-huh."

The ranger hung his head, and then looked up and over to the outlaw. "Then what is it?"

"Why didn't you ask?...It's Pickens."

"Easy's brother?" asked Loraine.

"Uh-huh…All of us."

"What do you mean, all of us?" asked Bodie.

"Think he means the whole gang are brothers," said Padrino.

"Uh-oh," muttered Bone.

Slick started nodding at the different bodies. "That's Easy, course…Shorty there, Fats behind the rock an' Earl down near the crick."

"No Slim?" asked Bone with a grin.

"Naw, Fats was till he outgrowed it, then become Fats."

"Any more of you?" inquired Loraine.

"Uh-uh…Jest Big Daddy an' Uncle Fester."

"Where's the homeplace?" asked Bodie.

"Jest outside of Goshen."

"Where's that?" Loraine looked at Bodie.

"Southeast of Paradise, 'bout six miles or so."

"Land of Goshen," said Padrino.

"Say what?" replied Bodie.

"In the Bible, it's where the Jews lived before Moses led them out in the Exodus. The Egyptian's gave it to them to live when they were slaves because many of the Jews raised sheep. 'Ye may dwell in the land of Goshen; for every shepherd is an abomination unto the Egyptians.'...*Genesis 46:34*," said Padrino.

"They's a lot of folks 'round Goshen what raise sheep, too," added Slick. "There's the other horses." He nodded at four of them tied to some persimmon saplings.

Thirty minutes later, they had the four bodies tied over their saddles, and Slick astride his horse as everyone, but Padrino, headed toward Paradise, some two miles to the southwest.

PARADISE, TEXAS

Gunn McQueen stepped out of the Western Union and Cable office two doors down from the Horse Head Saloon and started to untie his mount from the hitching rail. He turned his head to the sound of a rinky-tink piano banging out *Sweet Rosie O'Grady*, a popular tune of the time.

"Ah, what the hell."

He wrapped his lead back around the rail, turned and walked the fifty feet to the nine-foot high double doors in the middle of the saloon.

Gunn opened the right side and then pushed through the batwing doors used during the spring and summertime when it was warmer.

After letting his eyes adjust to the dim light put out by the seven coal oil lamps mounted on a wagon wheel suspended by a rope from the fourteen foot high embossed tin ceiling and single lamps at each end of the bar, the 5'8" Gunn sauntered inside like a banty rooster. He bellied up to the ornate bar.

"What'll it be, mister?" asked the smallish balding barkeep in a once-white collarless shirt with black garters holding the too-long sleeves up from his hands. "Name's Percy."

"Beer."

Percy filled a mug and set it in front of Gunn who responded by placing a nickel beside it.

"Thank you, much," said the bartender as he moved down the way to serve a couple of other customers.

Bone, Loraine and Bodie rode into the north side of the small agrarian town with their prisoner and the four bodies in tow.

"That's the constable's office down at the end of the block," said Bodie. "Got no idea where the undertaker's place is."

They pulled rein in front of the small brick building, dismounted and tied up. The sign over the doorway simply read: CONSTABLE'S OFFICE.

"Well, that's efficient."

"Wait till you meet the constable, Bone," said Bodie as he pushed the door open.

The short, rotund peace officer in a snug-fitting three piece suit sat behind a battered oak desk going over some paperwork that appeared to have several columns of figures on it. The round-faced, bespeckled, German looked up.

"Vas is dis?" He removed his wire-rimmed glasses.

"You need ze appoint..." he stopped talking, got to his feet and pointed at Bodie. "You are ze Texas Ranger Bo...Bo..." He searched for the name.

"Texas Ranger Bodie Hickman, Mister Muller. This is Deputy Sheriff Bone and his wife, Deputy Sheriff Loraine Bone."

"Oh, ya, ya, it's Constable Muller…Vat can I do for you?" He looked at Slick. "This is prisoner, ya?"

"Ya…Uh, yes, need to put him in your lockup till the county sheriff can get over here."

"Oh, zat is not possible. Zer is no one to guard him."

"Looks like you get the job, sunshine," said Bone.

"I am not ze Sunshine, I am ze Constable."

"Exactly," said Bodie.

"But, I vouldn't be able to go eat dinner."

"Breakin' my heart," muttered Bone.

"We'll have Cookie Magruder bring something down from the Red Robin," said Bodie.

"But, who vill pay for ze feeding of ze prisoner?"

"The city of Paradise…I would suspect," replied Bodie.

"It is not in ze budget," he whined.

"Not our problem, this is official Texas Ranger business until the sheriff gets here from Decatur…We also have four bodies outside draped over their horses. Where is the undertaker located?"

"Vat did zey die from?"

"Lead poisoning," answered Loraine. "They were dumb enough to try to rob us at our camp earlier."

"Vat are zer names?" He got out a pad and a pencil, he looked up, ready to write.

"The Pickens brothers...Easy, Fats, Shorty, and Earl. This one here is Slick," said Bodie. "Book 'im on attempted murder of a peace officer."

The color drained from his pinkish face. "Oh, zis is not goot, not goot at all...Ze father and uncle vill not be happy, not happy at all." He took out a white handkerchief and mopped his suddenly sweating forehead.

Bone leaned over and put his huge hands on the little fat man's desk. "Tell you what do, Constable, you tell them the boys will be at the undertakers and that we headed down to the Brazos canyons, if they want to talk about it."

"Oh, it's not ze talking zey vill vant to do...No, not at all."

"Whatever...Where's the undertaker's office?" asked Bone.

The pale constable pointed to the south. "Down zat vey, two blocks."

"Thank you," said Loraine. "Do you mind if we put this one in your cell, so we can have our handcuffs back?"

"Ya, ya." He got to his feet and shuffled back to the two empty cells and opened the first one.

Bodie shoved Slick forward and inside the steel-strapped door, turned him around and unlocked the cuffs with the key Bone had handed him and closed the door behind him.

"Thanks for your help, Constable…Oh, I'd lock that if I were you." He nodded at the cell door behind him.

Muller's jowls shook as he nodded and watched Bodie, Bone and Loraine exit his front door.

Twenty minutes later, they trotted their horses back up the street after dropping the bodies off at the Archebald Undertaking Parlor.

"Anybody for a beer before we head back out to the camp? Padrino only said not to get rooms," said Bodie.

A big grin spread across Bone's face. "Thought you'd never ask."

They reined over to the hitching rails in front of the Horse Head, dismounted and tied up. There were numerous nondescript horses out front, most standing hip-shot and asleep.

Bone opened the right side tall front door and pushed the batwings open for Loraine and Bodie to enter, and then he followed.

Loraine shook her head as they stood there for a moment letting their eyes adjust to the light. "Uh-huh, smells like the rest of 'em...stale beer, cheap liquor, tobacco spit, smoke, vomit, and urine."

"You were expecting maybe lilacs and daffodils, Pard? It's like George Strait's song, *Every Little Honky Tonk Bar*," quipped Bone as he turned and met the gaze of a small beady-eyed young man in a black plainsman's hat and twin ivory-handled Colts strapped low on his hips. "Uh-oh."

The young gunhawk's eyes got big as saucers as he studied who walked in the door, and then they squinted down to slits.

§§§

CHAPTER SEVENTEEN

WAGGONER BRANCH

Padrino was freshening his coffee when he heard a slight sound in the bushes. Thinking first it was a coon searching around the camp for scraps, he set the pot back down and returned to his rock seat.

More sounds.

"Umm, too much racket for a coon or possum," he muttered.

Padrino closed his eyes and concentrated on the area where the movement was coming from. He opened them and focused on the darkness at the edge of camp, surreptitiously pulled his small tac light from his BDUs and abruptly flicked it on in wide-beam on the area.

Two large eyes, just a little over four feet off the ground, showed red in the glow of the light. A slight squeal came from the creature.

With a speed that belied his age, Padrino shot to his feet, dropping his cup and sprinted to the tree where he saw the eyes peering at him from behind it. He completely illuminated the area with his powerful LED flashlight.

A dirty-faced, scraggly-haired child in rags, no more than five or six, was crabbing backwards on its hands and feet after falling in that position when Padrino shined the light.

"Whoa, child, wait a minute. I'm not going to hurt you. Just stop…Please, it's all right."

The ragamuffin stopped crabbing and sat down on the leaves covering the forest floor. The child's eyes were huge and the same color as Padrino's and Bone's—amber gold with bright golden flecks.

"Easy child, easy, now." He squatted down. "My name's Padrino, what's yours?"

The child shook its head.

"Can't talk?"

The child nodded.

"Don't want to, huh?"

Again, the nod.

He studied the waif a moment, looked at the rags, the face, and then smiled—*a girl.*

"Hungry?"

She licked her dry lips, tears came to her big eyes, and she nodded.

Padrino leaned forward and picked the skin and bones little girl up in his arms and hugged her to him. Instantly he saw the same visions he got when he touched the *moldivite* crystal and the golden disk Bone found.

He could feel her break down and her body rack with silent sobs as she hugged him back. He felt the wetness on his cheeks, but didn't know if it was from her—or his own. Padrino held her close for what seemed a long time, and then,

"You don't weigh fifty pounds, child and you're freezing...Come on, let's take care of that." He turned around and stepped back into camp and over to the fire.

Padrino set the shivering little girl on the rock he had been sitting on next to the blaze, grabbed a blanket from his bedroll and wrapped it around her tiny, frail body. He almost melted when her big gold eyes looked up at him with an obvious look of sheer gratitude.

"Thirsty?"

She nodded.

Fetching his canteen, he grabbed a clean cup, filled it about halfway and handed it to her. She held it with both hands and gulped it rapidly.

"Easy, honey, not too fast."

He pulled a white handkerchief from his pocket, wet it with more water from the canteen and gently began to wipe the dirt and tears from her face—then the grime from her briar-scratched arms and hands.

It was as moved her rag of a shirt, when he cleaned her neck, that he noticed a necklace, with a gold filigreed plate and a ruby embedded in a small disk in the center, almost identical to the one Bone found and on the statue. It was hung by a string of black onyx beads. *That's solid hammered gold...and a ruby, just like the disk.*

In a few moments, he sat back on his heels, looked at the almost black handkerchief and a shiny face and clean hands.

"Well, aren't you a cutie?"

She wrinkled her brow in confusion.

"You're very pretty," he said.

A tiny smile appeared across her face and more tears began to roll down her cheeks.

"No one ever said that to you before, I guess?"

She shook her head.

Padrino put some thick slices of bacon in a skillet and set it on a flat rock next to the fire where it began to sizzle. He opened a can of beans and put them in another pot and set it close.

She sniffed the air at the aroma of the cooking bacon and looked over in the skillet, and then up at Padrino and cocked her head in expectation.

"Now, while we're waiting on that to cook, have you ever had pickled peaches?"

She shook her head again.

He opened a can with his John Wayne can opener he'd had since he was in Marine Corps boot camp at Parris Island in 1960. He took out his

K-Bar knife and stabbed one of the whole, peeled peaches and placed it in a blue and white speckled graniteware plate. He laid a metal fork beside it and set it on another rock next her.

The little girl glanced at the fork, and then at the peach. She looked up at Padrino and he nodded to her and smiled. She grabbed the pickled sweet fruit in her right hand, held it to her mouth and took a bite.

Her already big eyes got bigger as she looked at him again and then tore into the peach in a frenzy.

"Easy, honey, there's plenty. Take your time, don't want to get sick."

Padrino turned the bacon over. "Do you have a name?"

She shrugged her bony shoulders and shook her tousled dirty blond hair.

"Well, let's just give you one, shall we?"

She nodded and finished the last of the peach, leaving only the pit.

"How about...uh...I know, Melisande? It means honey bee, strength and determination...We can call you Milly for short?"

Her eyes sparkled and she finally smiled.

"We need to get you some clothes…Hmm, let's see." He closed his eyes and directed his thoughts at Lucy for a couple of moments and finally looked up at Milly and smiled. "Well, we'll see what happens…Looks like the beans and bacon are ready."

He scooped some of the beans into her plate and added all four of the thick slices of smoke-cured fatback to her plate and handed it back to her.

She picked up a piece of the crisp bacon and took a bite. Again her eyes went wide and she put the entire piece in her mouth and chewed.

"Slow down, eat it slowly, Milly…Here, look." He took the fork and scooped some of the steaming red beans on it and held it in front of her face.

She opened her mouth and he inserted the fork, she closed it and he withdrew the utensil so she was able to chew the cooked, seasoned legume. Once more a look of surprise and pleasure came across her face.

Padrino placed the handle of the fork in her tiny hand, showed her how to hold it and use it to feed herself. She quickly adapted and picked up the technique and began almost shoveling the food in her mouth.

Padrino smiled. "Easy, baby, there's plenty…Take your time."

She looked up at him with what only can be described as unconditional love, nodded and continued more slowly.

HORSE HEAD SALOON

Bone grinned and focused on Gunn McQueen until the young man finally turned back around to the bar to attend to his beer.

"What is it, Bone?" asked Loraine.

"That little squirt at the bar, that thinks he's a new version of Billy the Kid is one of the bunch that's following us."

"How do you know?" asked Bodie.

Bone just looked at him. "Trust me, Ranger…Probably too late, but pretend you don't see him." He suddenly jerked and froze in place.

"What?" asked Loraine.

"Lucy…I feel Lucy, but she wants me to get clothing for a small child…smaller than her."

"Why?" Loraine looked at him.

"Damn if I know. Wonder if the mercantile is still open?"

"One way to find out," she replied.

Bone turned to Bodie. "Watch yourself, we'll be back in a bit."

The ranger grinned. "Been here before, Bone. Take your time."

He and Loraine turned around and went back out the door.

Bone and Loraine walked the half-block to Milstead's Mercantile. There were still lamps burning inside and they could see what was most likely the proprietor at the cash register, removing and counting the daily receipts.

They tried the door, but it was locked. The owner looked up, shook his head and mouthed 'Closed'. He went back to his daily chore of counting receipts.

Bone held up his badge against the glass in the top half of the nine-foot tall entrance. "Hope he can't read it from that distance," he said as he put it back in his possibles bag.

The man held up one finger, put a stack of bills back in the register, headed to the door and unlocked it. "How can I help you officer?"

"I'm Deputy Sheriff Bone and this is my wife Deputy Sheriff Loraine Bone…We're actually from Jacksboro and find ourselves in need of some things before we head back out of town."

"Jacksboro? Interesting. I suppose so, come on in. What is it you require?…I'm Carl Milstead, the owner."

They walked inside toward the main counter. The store smelled faintly of cedar floor sweep and lavender soap.

"Thank you, so much, Mister Milstead, this won't take a moment. We need some clothing for a young girl…say five or six."

Milstead had a puzzled expression on his face. "Five or six, you say?" He walked back toward the rear wall, occasionally glancing over his shoulder. "Here we are, help yourselves, I'll be at the front counter." He turned and walked away.

"That was easier than I thought," said Loraine.

"Right." Bone looked at her. "Okay, pick some stuff."

"Me?"

"You're the woman…What do I know about buyin' little girl's clothing?"

"And you think I do?" She turned and started going through the clothing.

"Well, you were one…once."

She glared at him briefly, and then started with some undergarments, picked up some socks and added a couple of day dresses, a night gown, and a sweater."

"Better get a warm coat, might turn off cold."

"Right." She nodded and picked out a dark green wool cape with a hood.

"Good choice, Pard."

"It's something I might have liked when I was little."

"You're still little to me…Don't forget shoes…and my gut tells me, a blanket."

"Oh, of course." She picked a dark blue wool blanket with a white stripe across the center and a pair of ankle-high lace ups. "Hope these fit…All right, that should do it."

They walked to the front counter and laid the clothing, blanket and shoes on top.

"That be all?" asked Milstead. "What about some toiletries?"

Bone and Loraine exchanged glances.

"Good idea," she said.

He gathered a hairbrush and comb set with a small mirror from behind him, set the items beside the clothing and began to add everything up.

"Dollar ten, plus three, plus two fifteen, two dollars twice and ninety cents…That comes to eleven dollars and fifteen cents."

Bone laid a ten and a five dollar bills on the counter. "Here, keep the change for the trouble."

"Oh, no trouble at all, sir."

"That's all right keep it anyway."

"Thank you, sir," he said as he wrapped the items in some brown wrapping paper and tied the bundles with string. "Here you are folks." He walked around the counter. "I'll let you out."

"Thank you, Mister Milstead, you've been very accommodating," said Loraine.

They walked back down the boardwalk, stopped at the horses and put the smaller items in their saddlebags and tied the blanket behind Bone's cantle. Then they turned to the Horse Head Saloon and entered.

"Oh, damn, might have known," said Bone.

§§§

CHAPTER EIGHTEEN

WAGGONER BRANCH

Padrino took Milly's plate that she had wiped with a piece of leftover hot water cornbread and set it on the other side of the fire. "Clean it later."

She pulled the blanket tighter around her while her doe-eyes watched Padrino's every move.

"Feel better, now, Milly?"

She gave him a wan little smile and nodded.

"Still hungry?"

Milly shook her head.

"Do you live around here?"

She shrugged her thin little shoulders, shook her head and a sad look washed over her face.

"Do you know where you came from?"

Milly raised her left arm from inside the blanket and pointed in a general southerly direction.

"That's a really pretty necklace, did you bring it from your home?"

She nodded.

"Was it a gift or did you find it?"

She shrugged.

"You found it?"

Milly nodded again.

"Do you have a mother and father?"

She shook her head and started to cry again.

"I'm sorry, does it hurt thinking about them?"

Milly pursed her lips and stared into the fire.

"I'm sorry, honey," he said.

She got to her feet, stepped over to Padrino and wrapped her arms around his neck and hugged him tightly while the tears flowed again.

For the first time Padrino could remember, he was at a complete loss as what to say or do next.

HORSE HEAD SALOON

Bodie and Gunn McQueen were faced off less than ten feet apart in front of the bar. The tension in the room was palpable.

Loraine stepped forward past Bone before he could do anything. "Are you picking on the little guys again, Bodie?"

Gunn wheeled in her direction. "I ain't no little guy, woman, you watch your mouth."

She grinned. "No, you're not little compared to a child, but to a man, you are...Why, you're not hardly any bigger than me."

"Damn you, woman, I ain't little!"

"Why, of course you are, my husband here could use you to shine his boots with. Matter of fact, I probably could too."

"Pard, I don't think..."

She held up her hand to the side for Bone to stop.

"I'll show you who can shine boots, split-tail." He started to step toward Loraine.

"Oh, I really wish you hadn't said that, now I'm going to have to hurt you."

Bodie got a look of concern on his face while Bone's face took on his enigmatic grin.

"Loraine, I got this…"

She held her other hand to Bodie as Gunn stepped up to her.

"Now, bitch, I'm going to show…"

That was as far as he got as Loraine slapped him back and forth across his face six times before he could blink, staggering him back.

He put his left hand to his face and drew the ivory-gripped Colt on his right side. His thumb was pulling the hammer back when Loraine's left foot whipped up in a roundhouse kick, knocking it out of his hand, up in the air behind and to her right.

Bone snatched the .45 in midair as it arced up in front of his face. He thumbed the loading gate open, spun the cylinder with his index finger and unloaded the revolver—the rounds skittered and bounced off the barroom floor. He pitched the weapon over to the bar top.

"What the…?" said the stunned gunman.

Loraine stepped back up and slapped him six more times across the face. She moved back, did a reverse kick with her right foot and sent his hat sailing over behind the bar.

Before she set her foot to the floor, she brought it back across the left side of his face, spinning him around and to the ground. The move mimicked her back and forth slaps with her hand, but it was with her moccasin-sheathed foot.

The gunman wobbled to his feet while a grinning Loraine stood over him, her arms folded over her bosom. Both sides of his face glowed a bright pink. He went for his right-hand Colt, realized it wasn't there, and started to reach for his left.

Loraine raised her right knee and snap-kicked the young gunhawk five times in the face with the bottom of her foot, in less than one and a half seconds, staggering him back with every strike as she hopped forward on her left with each kick. Blood spurted from his mangled nose.

She reached out, removed his left hand gun, and pitched it over her head to Bone. He caught it, unloaded it the same way he had the first, and flipped it back to her.

Loraine jammed it in his holster and slapped him four more times. Then she drove the heel of her hand under his chin, making his teeth click together audibly, and dropping him to the floor like so much dirty laundry.

Bone leaned over and said to Bodie, "I love that woman."

Bodie's chin was on his chest.

"You can breathe, now," said Bone to the ranger with a grin as he nudged him with his elbow.

Loraine turned and walked back over to her husband and Bodie.

Gunn slowly staggered to his feet. "Damn, what'd she hit me with?" He blinked his eyes, shook his head, and then drew his left hand Colt, thumbed the hammer back and pulled the trigger in Loraine's direction. It clicked on an empty chamber—they were all empty.

Bone smashed him on top of the head with an overhead hammer fist, dropping him back to the floor, out cold. "She hit you with a sample, jerk…and that was some more."

Bone, Loraine and Bodie turned and headed out the door to their horses and mounted up.

"Well, let's go see what Padrino's been up to…I got a feeling," said Bone.

They trotted their horses down the street with Bodie's eyes glued on Loraine and a wry grin on his face.

WAGGONER BRANCH

Bone, Loraine and Bodie rode into the picket area next to the campsite on the creek, dismounted and pulled their tack. They walked the short distance over to the camp.

Padrino and Milly were lying against his saddle when they walked in. The child rolled over and hugged him when she saw Bone and the others enter the camp. They exchanged 'aha' glances knowingly when they saw the little girl.

"My Padrino," she said, protecting him with her tiny body.

"You can talk." He looked down at the little waif wrapped about him.

"Uh-huh." She looked fearfully over her shoulder at the big man, Loraine and Bodie.

"Strangers."

"No, baby, they're friends...the big guy is Bone, he's my godson, the pretty lady next to him is his wife, Loraine, and the redheaded fellow is a Texas Ranger. His name is Bodie." Padrino got to his feet with Milly straddling his hip. "Guys, this is Milisande or Milly for short." He set her on the ground in front of him, but she turned and hugged his legs.

Loraine walked over and squatted down in front of her. "You know what, honey? We bought you a bunch of new things. Would you like to see them?"

She looked up at Padrino. He smiled and nodded to her.

Loraine glanced back over her shoulder at Bone for him to bring the parcels. He brought them over and set them all behind his wife.

Milly released her grip on Padrino and turned to face Loraine as she opened the first package, took out the dresses and held them up.

The child took one of the dresses held it to her and then looked back at Loraine and burst into tears.

Loraine took her in her arms and held her tight as the child cried. She looked back at Bone and her own eyes were full as she mouthed, 'Oh, wow', to him.

Bone turned away to hide his own tears.

Loraine then showed her the other dress, the undergarments, shoes and the cloak. "But, honey, we need to go down to the creek and wash up before we try on these nice things, all right?"

Milly leaned back, looked at Loraine's brown eyes and nodded.

"I was hoping you'd suggest that," said Padrino.

Milly turned and grabbed his hand. "My Padrino come?"

He grinned. "No, baby, let Loraine take you down and get you all washed up. I'll be right here."

"I need a quick pot of warm water, Padrino. I'm not going to dunk this child in that ice cold creek water. I've got some towels in one of the panniers, Bone. Get them for me and a bar of that lavender soap."

"Got it done, Babe." He headed over to the stack of supplies, fished out two towels and brought them back to his wife.

Padrino had already stepped over to the creek and dipped up a full pot of water. He brought it back and set it on a flat rock next to the fire while Loraine was showing Milly the rest of the clothes.

Thirty minutes later, Loraine led the child back into camp in her new night shirt. Her blond hair was still damp, but, clean and brushed out.

"My goodness is that the same child?...It's Princess Milisande," said Padrino as he knelt down when Milly rushed over to him and threw her arms about his neck.

He looked up at Loraine, with tears in his eyes and said softly, "Thank you."

Loraine had to bite her lip to keep from her voice breaking. "You're welcome. It was a pleasure. She's a dream."

"It's time for you to go to bed, little one," said Padrino.

"Bodie and I made her a bed of cut cedar branches and got another blanket for her. We built it next to your bedroll, Padrino, so she can be close to you...I think she's bonded," commented Bone.

He looked up and nodded. "We both have."

Padrino held her hand and walked her over to the bed and tucked her in. He sat down beside her and pulled her top blanket tight under her chin and began to softly sing *Brahm's Lullaby*, "Lullaby and goodnight, with roses bedight, With lilies o'er spread is baby's wee bed. Lay thee down now and rest...may thy slumber be blessed..." Padrino looked closely and saw her even breath and her sweet face relax as she drifted off to sleep.

He got to his feet and softly stepped back over to the fire, poured himself a cup of coffee and sat down on his rock. "Well, it's been quite a night."

"You could say that. I think yours was more interesting than ours...You go first," said Bone.

§§§

CHAPTER NINETEEN

WAGGONER BRANCH

"...an' she never even broke a sweat. I was flummoxed, I'm here to say...Ain't never seen the like." Bodie took another sip of his coffee as he finished the story of their town adventure.

"That's why I let her do my heavy fighting," said Bone.

Loraine whacked him across his chest with her arm.

"Sounds like he was all hat and no cattle," commented Padrino with a smile.

"Oh, he was deadly enough," added Bone. "That's why I took the bullets out of his shooters."

"Wonder what he's goin' to tell the others when he gets back to their camp?" pondered Bodie.

"Probably that he was ganged up on," said Loraine. "He's sure going to be angry, though."

"Well, my daddy always told me when I was playin' football, 'Bone, you want to beat the fella in front of you...just get him mad'...Trust me, it works." He grinned.

"Wonder what's had Milly so traumatized?" asked Loraine.

"My gut tells me she lost her parents in some tragic way, house fire, outlaws...something horrendous," said Padrino. "Think maybe we'll find out in the morning after she's had a good night's sleep on a full stomach...and knowing there's someone to protect her."

"She was crying out for love and solace…She's really so sweet," commented Loraine.

"Where do you think she got that necklace?" inquired Bodie.

"She indicated that she found it," replied Padrino. "I think it came from the same source as did the statue…the *Paracas*." He glanced at Bone. "Our ancestors…My gut also tells me that she may be descended from them…like we are. I got the same visions from the disk as when I first picked her up and held her."

"Yeah, her eyes, too," agreed Bone, nodding. "Didn't you say that her home was south of here?"

Padrino nodded. "She pointed in the direction of the Brazos canyons."

"Well, we'll see what tomorrow brings, but for now, I think I'll pay our friends a little visit," commented Bone.

"Where do you think they're camped?" asked Bodie.

"A little over a mile upstream, on the other side," Bone replied.

"How do you know? Did you have a vision too?" asked Bodie.

Bone shook his head and grinned. "Saw a campfire flickering through the woods when we rode up. Thought it was a lightnin' bug, till I realized they're not around this time of year."

"Oh, right," the ranger replied.

"Riding?" asked Padrino.

"Nope, like I said, it's only a mile or so. I can cover that a lot easier and quieter on foot." He got to his feet, checked his .50 caliber and headed into the darkness. "Laterbye."

"You be careful, you big lug," said Loraine.

Bone stopped and looked over his shoulder. "I was born careful, baby doll."

"I know better," Loraine said as he disappeared into the night lit only by the light of the stars and a horned moon.

Fifteen minutes later, Bone slipped up through the brush on the upwind side of the horses and paused under a large holly tree just outside the ring of light cast by the campfire of the three men following them.

He touched two of the runic type symbols engraved in gold in the turquoise-like stones set in solid gold links that completely encircled his thick wrist.

The night air around him shimmered briefly as what little light there was bent around him, rendering him virtually invisible.

Lucy had the electronic bracelet made especially for Bone after she was rescued by her space-faring race of humanoids in 2014—one hundred and seventeen years after her spacecraft crashed at Aurora, Texas in 1897.

They had been visiting Earth for millennia and were dubbed the *Anunnaki*—meaning sky gods—by the *Sumerians* over five thousand years ago.

Bone moved softly out from under the tree, closer to the outlaw's camp, being careful where he stepped. Even though invisible to the naked eye, he would still leave tracks and whatever noise he made would easily be heard. *Love these Apache moccasins Bass Reeves gave me,* he thought, referring to the knee-high soft leather footwear on his feet.

He stepped carefully into the camp proper and stood near their campfire, making sure he was on the upwind side as any smoke would reveal his presence.

"You damn little shit, I told you to stay out of the saloon," said Ace.

"You're not daddy, so leave me alone," snapped Gunn.

"If I were, I'd whip you till you couldn't stand..." commented his older brother as he looked at Gunn's swollen nose, black eyes and fat lip. "Looks like somebody did that for me anyway."

"Told you a bunch of 'em jumped me...but I seen them folks we've been tailin'...least that man-mountain an' his wife."

"What about the ranger?" asked Ace.

"Uh...yeah, he wuz there too," answered Gunn.

"They didn't know who you wuz, did they?"

"Uh...No...no, fact is they left 'fore I got jumped on. You know how some cowboys treat fellers smaller'n them...But, I left my mark on several of 'em."

Ace looked askance at his little brother. "Right."

"It's the truth! Would I lie?"

"Yeah, you would."

"Shhh," said the half-breed. "John Horse smell another white man." He cocked his head, looked all around and peered at the darkness surrounding the camp.

"Do what?" asked Ace.

"Smell another white man. Injuns know."

"Oh, bull, you probably smell whatever guys it was that jumped on Gunn."

"Unnn, meby so." He scanned the night again. "Meby not."

Bone grinned and then slowly stepped over to one of the saddles at the edge of the light with someone's bedroll. He took out his 3.5 inch black Benchmade 154CM razor-sharp knife, wrapped his big hand around it to hold the blade and pressed the release button. He slowly relaxed his fingers allowing the blade to open and lock into position.

Bone looked back at the three men once more, moved to the billet side away from the fire and eased the cinch up in his hand. He sliced through over two-thirds of the wool strands of the cinch that were woven around the steel O ring attached to the leather billet on the right side of the saddle, grinned and rose to his feet. *Wonder whose saddle it is? Hope it's the little turd's.*

He reached in his parfleche and pulled out a handful of rough walnut-sized stones and spread them around underneath one of the unrolled blankets. *That oughta be comfortable.* He slipped back into the darkness where he turned his bracelet off and headed back toward camp.

"You reckon they'll be movin' out tomorrow, Horse?" asked Ace.

"Uhh, should…We follow," said the half-Comanche as he again studied the darkness.

Bone slipped quietly back into the camp. "Any coffee left?" he asked as he stepped out of the darkness.

Bodie jumped. "Dang, Bone, you could give us a little warnin'."

"Thought I was making plenty of noise coming up."

Padrino grinned. "Heard you five minutes ago when you crossed the creek."

Bone looked at Bodie. "See."

Loraine poured him a cup of coffee and handed it to him.

"Thanks, babe." He sat down on a large cottonwood log that had washed down the creek at one time.

"Well?" asked Bodie.

"Like we figured, his story wasn't quite the same as ours...Fact is, he just barely mentioned we were there, but didn't know who he was." He chuckled. "All that was before half the saloon jumped him, but he managed to fight 'em off, was his explanation for his banged up face."

"What did you do to them?" asked Loraine.

"Oh, let's just say one of them will find his bedroll is not too comfortable and tomorrow another will probably fall off his horse at some time or another...saddle and all."

"Put rocks under one of their blankets, didn't you?" asked Padrino. "...and cut someone's cinch?"

Bone shrugged. "It could happen...They got a half-breed tracker with them, not that we're being hard to track," he added. "He was kind of like Bass...he could smell me. The brothers passed it off as the guys that tangled with the younger one left their scent on him." He shook his head.

"Don't know about ya'll, but I think I'm ready to turn in," said Padrino.

"Sounds good to me...Ready, short cakes?" asked Bone.

"I am," Loraine answered.

"Ya'll go ahead, I'll bank the fire and get fresh water for the coffee pot," said Bodie. "See ya'll in the mornin'."

A mocking bird serenaded the camp with his repertoire of songs. He was joined by a bright red male and a brown female cardinal singing back and forth as the sun peeked over the ridge to the east.

Bone was first up. He eased into the woods to drain his full bladder, and then walked over to the fire pit, stirred the coals to life and added some small sticks.

The shrill cry of a hunting majestic bald eagle pierced the morning quiet as he glided on a thermal looking for his breakfast below in the clear water of the creek. Abruptly, he folded his wings and dove down like a bullet, opening and flaring them just above the water, and then extending his long wicked claws toward the water.

There was a momentary splash as he hit the still surface and then with mighty thrusts of his powerful wings, he beat his way back up to his domain with a four pound bass clutched in one foot. The monarch of the sky headed off to his nest, to share the meal with his mate sitting on three eggs.

Bone watched the perennial struggle of life and death in nature and smiled. "And so it continues," he muttered as he added larger pieces of wood to the fire.

Loraine joined him and held her hands out to the burgeoning blaze. "Feels good…Morning husband." She kissed him on the lips as he bent over. "Love you."

"Love you too, babe. The water should be getting hot."

"Okay." She dug into the poke sack near the pit and pulled out the five pound cloth bag of ground Arbuckles coffee, took two handfuls and added them to the pot. "Be ready in a jiffy."

A bloodcurdling scream suddenly echoed through the camp—Milly.

Padrino jumped to his feet, still in his longjohns, and looked around just as she latched her arms around his legs holding tight to him, screaming, "Injun! Injuns!"

§§§

CHAPTER TWENTY

WAGGONER BRANCH

Padrino knelt down and hugged Milly. "It's all right, honey, you're safe. It's all right...Shhhh." He comforted the sobbing child.

She sniffed as her body continued to jerk with emotion, and then she nodded.

"Can you tell me what happened, Milly?"

The others had gathered around, each showing concern on their faces.

"Do you remember?" Padrino asked.

"Uh-huh." She sniffed again. "Injuns attacked our farm...Killed momma an' daddy." Milly managed to blurt out before bursting into tears again.

"Shhh, baby, it's all right now." He held her tight and let her cry it out.

Finally she stopped enough to continue, "They burned our house an' barn...I...I hid down in a cave...by the creek...till they left." She caught her breath and sniffed again.

Loraine leaned over with a clean handkerchief, wiped her eyes and let her blow her nose. She looked at Padrino, he nodded and lifted Milly up to Loraine's arms. The frail little body continued to jerk as the memories flooded back.

Padrino nodded to Bone and Bodie. They stepped over to the fire.

"What do you make of that, Bodie?" asked Padrino.

The big ranger shook his head. "That's the thing, Padrino, there hasn't been any Injun trouble since

Quanah Parker surrendered the last of the Comanche to Colonel Mackenzie at Fort Sill in '75...that I know 'bout."

"Renegades?" questioned Bone.

"Possible...The Brazos canyons was a real mecca for Injun tribes an' outlaws on the scout for many years. Mason said they took whole companies down in there when he was still in the cavalry...I suppose there could be a few Comanch or Kiowa left there...still hidin'. Don't see how, though."

"She saw something that totally traumatized her. I believe that," said Padrino.

"Wonder if we can get hold of the girls and have them do a Google search for Indian activity in the late 1800s in Texas?" suggested Bone.

"What's a Google?" asked Bodie.

"It's like being able to access a whole library with all sorts of information, including newspapers, on that television thing we've mentioned before, called the Internet...Kinda handy," replied Bone.

"I can imagine," said Bodie.

"Worth a shot," answered Padrino.

He pulled his *moldivite* crystal from the large side pocket of his camo BDUs and handed it to Bone. "Here, hold this close to my cell and I'll see if I can get through." Padrino removed his Galaxy 9 phone from his back pocket and looked at it. "Well, what do you know, have two bars...Glad you held my phone to your bracelet yesterday to charge off the crystal. Hard to believe it can do it in less than five minutes."

"Now if they're at the ranch, we could have something...If they're up, yet," said Bone as he nodded to Padrino.

The retired Marine Master Gunnery Sergeant speed dialed Peach and put his phone on speaker. One ring. Two rings.

"Hello," came a sleepy voice.

"Time to get up, Peach, need to go feed the chickens," said Bone.

"Okay, daddy, I'm up, I'm up." There was a long pause, then a screech came through the small speaker, "Bone, Bone, Bone. Oh, my goodness, that you?"

"No, Peach, it's Santa Claus, I'm looking for my elves," he replied.

"Stella! Stella, wake up, it's Bone and Padrino. Wake up."

In the background another sleepy voice could be heard. "What, what...Who?"

BONE'S RANCH
2018

"Where's Loraine?" Peach asked she asked as Stella, still in her PJs, stepped over from her bed, and jumped on Peach's.

"She's babysittin'," said Padrino.

"Doin' what?" the girls said together as they exchanged looks.

"Explain later. Need some info while we have a connection," answered Bone.

"What?" they said together again.

"Need you to Google and see if there was any hostile Indian activity in north Texas in the late 1890s...Now, girls, need it now," said Bone over the speaker.

"Right, right, honey-bunch. Give us a second," said Peach. "You know I don't function well before I've had my coffee."

She and Stella ran into Padrino's office and she tapped the spacebar on his desktop computer keyboard as she sat down in the antique sheriff style swivel chair. The screen instantly came to life and Peach opened a new tab.

"Alright, say again what you need, I'm at the keyboard…Go, buttercup," said Peach. "You need to see if there was any hostile Indian activity in north Texas an' what?"

"I'll go put the coffee on," said Stella.

"Bless you, girl," responded Peach.

"In the late 1890s," said Padrino through the speaker.

Peach's fingers flew over the keyboard and she hit *enter*.

"Thousand one, thous…Alrighty then, here we go…"

"What is it?" asked Bone.

"Give me a second, sugah…gotta read it first, then I'll give you the condensed version with the facts."

"Shades of Sergeant Joe Friday…Just the facts, ma'am," added Padrino with a grin.

"Small band of renegade Comanche, Apache and Kiowa Indians terrorize the north central Texas rural areas in and around Palo Pinto, Stephens, Erath and Parker Counties in 1898. The band was summarily eliminated by a Texas Ranger and several local sheriff deputies to terminate the threat to the rural populace of the area. One law officer was wounded in the action..."

Bone interrupted Peach. "Say who?"

There was another pause. "Reading, reading...nope, doesn't say."

"Anything else?" asked Padrino.

Peach scrolled the screen. "Uh...Don't see anything else, but a repeat of that phrase attributed to Texas Ranger Captain William 'Bill' McDonald in 1896 of 'One riot, one Ranger'...Actually it was said at an illegal prize fight between Bob Fitzsimmons and Pete Maher...Seems the mayor of Dallas met Captain McDonald and asked where the other Rangers were and McDonald replied, 'Hell, ain't I enough? There's only one prizefight!'."

"I didn't know that," said Bone.

"Now you do," commented Bodie.

"Was that Ranger Hickman?" asked Peach.

"Hi, ladies," said Bodie as he leaned toward the phone Padrino was holding up.

"Well, hello, darlin'," replied Peach.

"Here's the coffee, Peach," said Stella as she walked back into the ranch office with two cups, Tyrin was on her heels.

Peach took her cup, nodded a thanks and took a quick sip. "Say hi, to Ranger Hickman, Stella,"

"Oh, hey, Ranger."

"All right girls, we'll be in touch. Seems that as long as you're at the ranch near that statue and Padrino has his crystal…we should be able to get a connection," said Bone.

"What was that about Loraine babysittin'?" asked Stella.

"Long story, fill you in later…thankyoubye," said Bone as he disconnected.

"What in the world?" asked Stella as she looked at the screen.

"Honey, with Bone an' them…ain't no tellin'," said Peach.

WAGGONER BRANCH

"Forewarned is forearmed," said Padrino. "We just need to be sure to keep sweet Milly out of any danger…She doesn't need any more trauma."

"Well, it's not that we're goin' down there lookin' for renegade redskins, we're goin' to look for Padrino's treasure," said Bodie.

"But, they're apparently down there in that wilderness area and chances are they're in the canyons someplace…They could find us," added Bone.

Loraine walked up to the fire with Milly, who was wearing one of her new dresses, long black socks and her lace-up shoes. Her hair was brushed out and pulled up into dog-ears on each side of her head.

"Ooh, there is cuteness personified," said Padrino as he knelt down.

Milly stepped up and wrapped her arms around his neck. "My Padrino," she said as she hugged him.

"Yes, baby, I'm your Padrino." He kissed her forehead. "Hungry?"

"Uh-huh," she said with a smile.

"Feel better?" Bone asked.

She said, "Uh-huh. Had a…night…mare." Milly looked up at Loraine, who nodded.

"Do you think you can find where you used to live, Milly?" asked Bodie.

She shrugged. "I'm not sure. I was scared when I ran and hid…I never been away from home before."

"I know, baby," said Padrino as he hugged her again.

Loraine started breakfast. She put some oatmeal on to boil to go along with bacon.

"Ever had oatmeal, honey?" she asked as she sliced a couple of rashers from the slab.

"Uh-huh, I like it with sorghum or honey."

"Well, we've got sorghum," Loraine replied.

Milly smiled and nodded.

"Coffee's ready," said Bone as he flipped up the lid on the pot.

After breakfast, they broke camp and loaded up. Milly rode behind Padrino on his claybank gelding he had named, Star, because of the single white mark in the center of his forehead the size of a quarter.

Bodie led out leading the pack horse as before, followed by Loraine, then Padrino with Bone covering their back trail. It would be late evening by the time they reached the Brazos.

"Let's camp at that cave that we got here in," said Padrino.

Milly leaned to the side a little. "What do you mean, Padrino…got here in? How can you get here in a cave?"

"I'll try to explain it to you tonight, Milly, when we get there and maybe you'll recognize something nearby."

"I'll try. I just remember lots of woods an' cliffs an' creeks an' stuff. They all went down to the big river. There were bunches of caves…that's where I hid out every night."

"That where you found your pretty necklace?" he asked.

"Uh-huh."

§§§

CHAPTER TWENTY-ONE

JACK COUNTY

Ace, Gunn and John Horse continued to trail behind Bone's group around five miles.

Horse had ridden back to the others from up the trail. He turned and trotted his bay gelding alongside Ace. "Got white girl child with them now. Ride behind old man."

"Where'd she come from?" asked Ace.

"John Horse not know. Yesterday she no there…today she is."

"No matter…ain't gonna stop nothin'."

They followed the tracks down an embankment of a creek bed, across the shallow wet weather branch and started up the steeper south side. Gunn was behind Ace and Horse when he suddenly hollered.

"Hey! What the…" was all he got out before he hit the ground, saddle and all, and tumbled back into the water. "Son of a bitch!"

Horse and Ace reined up and turned in their saddles.

"What'n hell are you doin'?" asked Ace.

"Damnation!" Gunn got to his feet from the water and slung mud from his hands. He looked up at his brother. "Cinch broke."

"How the hell did that happen?…You must not have tied your latigo off."

Gunn picked up his saddle and pad and dragged them up out of the water to the bank and looked at the girth. "Naw, naw, it's tied off…busted loose on the other side."

"Aw, that cain't happen."

"Well, it did." He lifted the billet, and then the cinch. "Hell…been cut! Looky here."

He held up the billet that still had the O ring attached, and then the cinch showing over three quarters of the strands had been severed.

Ace and Horse rode back down the embankment and both dismounted.

"Lemme see that," said Ace stepping over beside his brother and grabbing the cinch.

"Damn, think you're right, little brother…Question is, how an' when?"

"It wuz awright when we unsaddled last night."

"But, not this mornin'…Don't make'ny sense."

"Meby was spirits Horse smelled last night."

The two brothers exchanged looks and then stared at the half-breed.

JACK COUNTY

"You say something if you recognize anything, all right?" Padrino said over his shoulder to Milly.

"I will."

"You covered a lot of ground, Milly...At least thirty miles. Do you remember when the Indians raided your farm?" asked Loraine.

"No, ma'am, not really...seems like a long time ago." She shrugged and shook her head. "I walked and walked...Ate berries, an' 'simmons when I could find 'em...Hid if I seen anybody."

"Why?" inquired Bone.

"I was scared."

"But, you weren't scared when Padrino found you," said Loraine.

"I was at first, but then he started talkin' to me an' I wadn't scared no more." She squeezed him tighter and leaned her cheek against his back. "I love my Padrino."

"I love you, too, honey...I will always protect you," he said.

"I know."

"Do you remember how many caves you hid in?" asked Bone.

"Uh-uh...Just a bunch."

Loraine nudged Sweet Face over next to Bone. "Think Milly's been on her own and walkin' for at least two months, considering, the distance she's covered, the condition of her clothes and the fact that she's so undernourished."

"Agreed, baby, as resourceful as she's been, it's dang lucky we found her when we did."

"God was watching out for that child and led her to us rather than to some nefarious characters."

"Yeah, they would have put some meat on her bones and sold her to the sex trade in Mexico."

"Especially being a blond," commented Loraine. "What are we going to do with her?"

"The way she's bonded with Padrino, don't think there's much choice."

Loraine nodded.

"See that ridge up yonder?" asked Bodie.

"Looks familiar," said Bone.

"Palo Pinto Mountains…That hogback is in Palo Pinto County," added Bodie. "Starts gettin' rough there…coolies, draws, gullies, creeks, and deep canyons. The Brazos started cuttin' through these mountains a long, long time ago."

"The cave we were transported here in is just on the other side of the ridge on the upslope from Rock Creek," commented Bone. "It flows into the Brazos…Deep canyon, but is all under Possum Kingdom Lake in our time."

"We can go through that saddle there in the ridge an' pitch camp near that cave ya'll were talkin' 'bout…Be dark soon," commented Bodie.

"Going to be raining soon, too, looks like," said Padrino, pointing at the dark cloud bank off to the northwest, over their right shoulders. "Need to find some shelter."

"You're right, Padrino, I hadn't noticed it," agreed Bodie. "Could be sleet, you know…That time of year."

"Guess I'm goin' to have to ride into Graford an' see as I can find you a new cinch an' send the boss man his telegram." Ace looked over at his brother, and then at John Horse. "Ya'll jest as well make camp. Don't think we'll lose them tracks…you, Horse?"

"No, follow easy…unless storm come."

"You mean like that one layin' back off to the northwest."

Horse and Ace turned to look at the dark blue line Gunn was talking about at the horizon.

"Aw, damn. Reckon I better git a hurry on…Could well be a cold front comin'. I make it to be five, six miles into town."

"An' that's five, six back, too," added Gunn.

"Know of any caves er 'bandoned farm houses in walkin' distance, Horse?"

"Used to be line shack over thataway." He pointed to the south.

"How far?" asked Gunn.

"Mile or so…meby. If still there."

"Worth a shot. You'll have to either tote yer saddle, little brother or walk 'longside yer horse an' hold it on his back."

"Ain't totin' it, you kin count on that."

"Figured." Ace reined his horse to the southwest. "Meet ya'll there." He kicked the bay gelding up into a lope.

PALO PINTO COUNTY

"Let's head to that saddle, I suspect we can find a cave fair quick," said Bodie as he nudged his line-back dun, Kiger Mustang, Lakota Moon, into a road trot.

"Hang on, baby." Padrino glanced over his shoulder at Milly as he bumped Tuck into a trot to match Bodie, Loraine and Bone.

Salt Creek was only belly deep on the horses where they crossed. Milly giggled as they splashed through the clear water and up on the far bank.

"Like that, did you?" asked Padrino.

"Uh-huh, it was fun."

"Well, there may be more fun later on."

"Oh, goodie."

They followed Bodie with the pack horse up the incline to the top of the hogback, and then down through the black jack oaks, cottonwoods, pecans and sycamores toward Rock Creek.

"Need to get to the other side of the creek before the storm hits. May play hob if it's a gully washer. Rock Creek can get pretty high an' rough, pretty quick," said Bodie.

"I'm sure our cave's on the other side. Had water on both sides when we drove in here in October, 2018…We crossed this creek when we walked out, didn't we, Pard?"

"It or one like it," Loraine answered.

"No question it's the one I crossed a few weeks back when I came," added Padrino. "I recognize that big outcrop over there on the other side…The cave is down that way about a half-mile."

"Believe you're right, Padrino…It looks so different in our time," said Bone.

"Lots of water will do that, they say," agreed Loraine.

They reined up at the bank of the creek.

"What do you think, Bodie?"

"Good a place as any, Bone."

"Lead out, then," said Padrino. "We're right behind you." He turned to Milly. "Be sure you keep your feet up, honey."

"I will."

They all glanced off toward the cloud bank which had filled almost a quarter of the sky in the last thirty minutes, and had a tinge of green to it.

"It's moving this way pretty fast," said Loraine as she nudged her mare into the water after Bone.

"Yeah, and looks like it's got some hail or sleet in it, too," added Padrino.

"Joy," commented Bodie as Moon's hooves grabbed purchase on the rocky bottom of the creek and pulled them out up on the bank.

"Have fun again, Milly?" asked Padrino as they joined the others on the bank.

"Yes, thank you."

"Which way?" asked Loraine.

"Six of one and half-dozen the other," answered Bone.

"Want to try for our cave?" inquired Padrino.

"What if it gets hit by lightning like with us?"

"Didn't *Anompoli Lawa* say it wouldn't be active till June during a blue moon, hon?"

Loraine glanced over at Bone. "What if he's wrong?"

"Then we may all wind up in 2018...or sometime," answered Bone.

"This baby doesn't need to be in a sleet or hail storm or freezing rain for that matter...regardless. We have to have shelter."

"Let's go then," said Bodie. "Lead on, Padrino, you know the way."

"Roger that." He squeezed Tuck to the left and worked up the incline a little and south along the creek.

In a few moments they spied the opening and moved up toward it.

Thunder rumbled across the northern sky as the churning, greenish-blue clouds boiled across the rocky landscape. Cloud to cloud lightning flashed, followed by a clap of more rolling thunder.

They dismounted in front of the opening.

"Think there's room in the back for the horses?" asked Bodie.

"I think so," replied Padrino as he helped Milly to the ground.

Lightning flashed and two seconds later was answered by another loud clap of thunder.

"Better hurry, gettin' close," said Bodie as he led Moon and the pack horse inside.

"Pard, you take Hildebrandt and I'll gather some wood from that blowdown over there."

"All right, baby."

Everyone was already in the cave and pulling their tack as Bone hurried to the entrance with a heavy armload of the cottonwood deadfall.

A downdraft of frigid air hit just as he got inside. A tremendous flash of lightning followed instantly by a deafening peal of thunder that literally vibrated the entire cliff, knocking dust from the ceiling.

"Jesus," exclaimed Bodie as the horses squealed in fear.

§§§

CHAPTER TWENTY-TWO

JACK COUNTY

John Horse and Gunn McQueen walked up to the abandoned one room shack and dismounted. There was a ramshackle lean-to on the side for horses.

Gunn slid his damaged saddle and pad from his mount's back, pushed the plank door to the cabin open and threw them inside. "I'll pull your tack, Breed, you go put the horses up inside that shed. Ain't no hay, so reckon they'll do without. Leastwise, be out of the weather."

"Unnn, Horse do."

He led Gunn's mount into the tiny shelter, tied him off, then came back and got his own and did the same as lightning flashed and thunder rolled overhead.

Tiny pellets of ice began to pepper the rusted tin roof of the shed and him as he ran toward the front door of the line shack.

"Ace no make it back before storm."

"Don't look like it...see any deadfall or anythin' we kin burn in that potbellied stove over there?" He nodded to the rusty heater in the corner.

Horse indicated a couple of broken chairs scattered about in the room. "Can start with those...See small pile of wood next to shack between here an' lean-to. Me get."

He headed back outside while Gunn gathered the broken pieces of chairs, put them in the stove and looked around the cabin for paper or something to serve as kindling. He spied what was left of an old Montgomery Ward Wish book. It had apparently been used for privacy papers in the outhouse and for starting fires in the stove before.

Gunn tore several pages from the worn catalogue, wadded them up and stuffed the balls of paper underneath the pieces of broken slat-back chairs inside the potbelly.

He pulled a match from his vest pocket, popped it with his thumbnail, watched it hiss, smoke and then flame up before he touched it to the dry paper. It instantly began to burn and in short order had caught the dry pieces of oak piled on top.

Horse came back inside with an armload of wood from the pile and a tree nearby that had blown down sometime in the past and threw it on the floor near the stove.

"Hnnn…get cold. Be hard night."

"Think Ace will make it back?"

"Not know. May wait out storm in town."

"Lucky bastard. Probably get some restaurant food an' spend a little time in a saloon with a sportin' gal."

"Uhhh…John Horse start some coffee. Little *pin-dah-lickyoee* cut bacon."

"Dammit, Breed, what have I said 'bout callin' me little?"

Horse looked at him with no change of expression and then continued filling the pot with water from his canteen.

BRAZOS CANYONS

Loraine had put the coffee on the rocks of the same fire pit she and Bone had used when they took shelter in the cave in 2018. It was only three months earlier, but seemed like a lifetime—and maybe it was.

"Wonder if we're still here?"

"Of course we're here, Bone, where else would we be?" said Loraine.

"I mean here…in this time."

"Wherever or whenever we are, Bone…it's here."

"Ya'll 're doin' it again," said Bodie.

Milly was sitting in Padrino's lap and looked up at the sage elderly man. "I don't understand, Padrino. What are they're talkin' about."

He grinned. "Well, we don't really know either, honey, we're just trying to be realistic…*Que será, será.*"

She frowned, cocked her head a little and looked up at him again.

"That means whatever will be, will be...Like you coming up on our camp."

"An' find you, my Padrino." She threw her arms around him.

"Yes, you did." He leaned back and looked at her gold-flecked eyes. "Do you remember your folks names?"

"Not very good. I think daddy's last name was Morrow...They said I was an orphan..." She began to tear up again. "I guess I am again."

"No, honey, you have me, now."

Milly nodded and hugged him tightly.

"Can you recall his first name?"

"Uh-huh...I think it was Tom."

"Tom?"

"Uh-huh, he was always sayin', 'Tom Morrow's gonna be a better day'."

Loraine glanced over at her from the fire pit and smiled.

"Oh, I see," said Padrino as he hugged her again.

Outside the entrance, which faced south, the sleet peppered down in swirling sheets past the opening as the wind blew from the north.

"It's a good thing we got to this cave when we did," commented Bodie.

"It would be miserable to be out in that. Bet it gets colder, too," added Bone.

Unknown to anyone in the cave, a pair of black eyes watched the entrance for a few moments from across the creek through the falling sleet, and then faded off into the brush.

"I'm willing to bet we didn't go anywhere unless they're having a storm in 2018 or whenever, at the same time," said Loraine as she stirred the beans and bacon.

"Good point, honey, didn't think about that…'Course, it could happen."

"Don't start," countered Bodie as he poured some hot coffee into his tin cup.

"Where do you want to start looking tomorrow, assuming the storm lets up?" asked Bone.

"Well, I'd say Sam Bass Holler's good a place as any," replied Bodie. "It's southeast of here."

The morning broke bright and cold. There was almost no wind, but the ground was covered with about three inches of sleet. It was going to be a sunny day.

Bodie stood at the entrance with his cup of hot morning coffee. Bone walked up beside him, also with a cup. Steam curled up from the hot trail brew from their cups into the cold air.

"What do you think?"

"Gonna be fine, Bone, be slick as a greased baby's butt on the slopes, but should be awright if we're careful."

"This is Texas, after all. We could have a warm front just as quick as that cold front…All this could be gone by tomorrow," said Bone.

"Think we should leave some of the supplies here?" inquired Loraine as she walked up behind the two men.

"Nope, may have to cover a lot of ground an' there's caves most everwhere along the river through these mountains," replied Bodie. "'Sides, this cave makes me nervous…somethin' 'bout it."

"Yeah, in our time we would say it has bad vibes," added Loraine.

"Feels kinda like walkin' through a graveyard at two in the mornin'…spooky, just plain spooky."

They turned and walked back inside and close to the fire to warm back up.

"Milly, do you remember crossing the big river at anytime?" asked Padrino.

"Uh-uh. There were some creeks an' streams, but didn't have to cross the big one…I don't think I could anyway, can't do anything more than dog paddle."

He looked at the others. "Well, both her folk's farm, and the cave where she found the necklace, are on this side of the Brazos."

"Uh-huh, the east and south side, I'd say. About fifteen miles all together, till the Brazos gets out of the Palo Pinto Mountains," agreed Bodie.

"Well, let's pack up, need to take the horses down to water first, then we'll be ready to head out," said Bone.

"Glad it didn't rain much, Rock Creek is still down," commented Padrino.

Bone, Loraine and Bodie led the five horses down to the creek and let them drink their fill of the clear cold water.

The big man shook his shoulders like a wet dog and frowned.

"What is it, honey?" asked Loraine as she watched him tense up.

He looked around and across the creek studying the rocks and brush areas intensely.

Without looking at her, he said sotto voce, "Got company, love."

§§§

CHAPTER TWENTY-THREE

JACK COUNTY

It was just past daybreak when Ace trotted up to the old line shack on his gelding through the coating of sleet. His tan canvas mackinaw was buttoned all the way to the top with the collar turned up and a black woolen scarf wrapped around his neck. He was accompanied by two big rough looking characters, Rufus and Mayhab 'Bear' Pickins.

The three men dismounted and pulled the plank door open, dragging the bottom across the three-foot wide stoop. The lower leather hinge had torn loose.

"Well, you made it out early, brother," said Gunn as he poured himself a fresh cup of coffee from the pot sitting on top of the potbellied stove. "Who's that with you?"

"Boss sent Rufus an' Mayhab Pickens from down near Goshen way. That group we're followin' killed four of Rufus' boys couple days ago an' put a fifth in the hoosegow…Mayhab here is their uncle." Ace indicated the giant bear of a man, well over six-five and three hundred pounds.

"How'd ya'll git hooked up?" asked Gunn.

"They was trailin' 'em, too. Seemed like the thang to do," said Ace. "Ya'll ready to ride?"

"Been waitin' on you. Figured you stayed over in Graford an' dipped yer wick down to the saloon."

"Passin' the time, little brother, passin' the time."

"Uh-huh."

"John Horse already watered the stock an' just wait on new girth to saddle little *pin-dah-lickyoee* horse."

Ace handed a brown paper wrapped bundle to the half-breed. "Found a used one...Then let's go an' see as we kin pick up their trail."

"Be easy in sleet," said Horse.

BRAZOS CANYONS

"Reckon it's that same bunch that's been doggin' us?" asked Bodie over his shoulder to Bone as he led off on a game trail south along the creek.

"No."

The horses stepped carefully through the slick sleet rapidly turning to mud as they trod alongside the waterway. The four riders loosened their handguns in the holsters and glanced around and across the creek apprehensively.

"Everbody stay alert, now," said Bodie.

By noon, they had reached a very rugged area where the Brazos curled back east on itself, creating a large horseshoe. There were some high cliffs to their left showing numerous caves and overhangs in the limestone rock with heavy woods on top at the crest.

"Looks like a good place to stop for a bite to eat an' give the horses a blow," commented Bodie as he reined up, slid from his saddle and stretched his legs.

"Not to say anything about our rear ends," added Loraine.

"Need a massage, babe?" asked Bone.

"Damn you, Bone…" She paused. "But on second thought, maybe later." Loraine winked at the big man.

"Anything around here look familiar, Milly?" asked Padrino.

She glanced up along the cliff and at the trees lining the plateau. "Uh-huh…I came down toward the river over there. I think our place is up yonder behind the trees at the top…But, daddy farmed some flat ground down closer to the river where it was easier to plow an' stuff."

Padrino stepped down, reached up, lifted the frail child from Star's back and set her on the ground.

"I hid in that cave up there." She pointed at a small opening along a narrow deer trail halfway up the face of the cliff.

"Is that where you found the necklace?" asked Bone as he loosened the girth on Hildebrandt.

She looked around, up the cliff, and then down a ways at the green, deep river moving its inexorable way south toward the gulf of Mexico, southwest of Galveston.

"Seems so long ago...almost like it was a dream." She fingered the gold plate at the bottom of the necklace.

Padrino also glanced around. "Pretty good place for an ambush, folks," said the old Marine.

"Everplace down here is, Padrino," replied Bodie looking carefully at the tree line at the crest.

"He's right," said Bone. "I'd say let's move a little closer to that rocky area to eat after Bodie and I water the guys...Better cover...Think we're being watched."

"We can go up the cliff and check out that small cave after we eat...Want to do that, Milly?" asked Padrino.

"Uh-huh." She nodded and gave him a hug.

The others also loosened their mount's cinches before handing the reins to Bone and Bodie to lead them down to the river bank.

Loraine carried the poke sack containing the supplies she would need to fix lunch.

Padrino held Milly's hand as they followed her over to the area with the boulders upbank from the water about twenty yards.

Bone and Bodie headed back toward the others when a shot ricocheted from a rock near Bone's foot. The horses squealed, danced to the side, and jerked back on the reins being held by the two men.

"Whoa, boys, whoa," said Bodie as he tried to calm the animals.

Loraine and Padrino looked up at the trees at the white smoke cloud drifting away in the breeze.

Padrino pushed Milly down next to the bottom of a boulder as he and Loraine rapidly drew their semiautomatic 1911As and snapped off three quick rounds each at the area around the smoke.

Bone and Bodie had settled the horses down enough to get them over to the shelter of the rocks and tie them to some saplings. They drew their weapons as they ran toward Loraine and Padrino's location.

"Our new friends, Bone?" asked Bodie.

He nodded. "I'd say…Good thing they're not too bright, waiting for us to stop."

"Maybe they were just waitin' for us to get to where they were an' didn't think about us stoppin' to eat."

"Good point," Bone said as another shot whined mournfully off down the river canyon from a rock nearby.

Bodie pitched Bone a Winchester and one to Padrino. "Managed to jerk these from the boots while we were tyin' up."

Bone hollered over to Loraine and Padrino. "On the count of three, lets fill that treeline with five shots each…Ready, one, two, three."

Bone jumped up with the rifle and worked the lever as fast as he could, firing at the top of the cliff while Bodie and Padrino did the same. Loraine tapped five from her Kimber that sounded like one shot, then everyone ducked back to cover.

Loraine popped a fresh magazine in her .45 when she got behind her boulder again.

They all exchanged glances as there was no return fire.

Bone held up his hand. "Wait…wait."

Padrino knelt down beside a whimpering Milly. "It's all right, honey. You're not hurt are you?" He brushed a blond curl from her forehead.

"Uh-uh…are you?"

"I'm fine, baby." He raised up a little. "Everybody all right?"

"I'm good," said Loraine.

"Me too," answered Bodie.

"Same," added Bone.

"I believe they're gone, people."

"Think you're right, Padrino. Don't sense anyone like before…Bodie, how about you and I take a little stroll up there and check it out."

"Let's go…Ya'll cover us," he said to Loraine and Padrino as he joined Bone.

"Like a blanket," commented Loraine as Bone handed her his rifle and pulled his .50 cal.

They worked their way up the steep slope to the top.

"You go right, I'll go left, Bodie."

"Got it."

With weapons in hand and cocked, the two law officers searched through the trees and limestone outcrops.

"Got one," said Bodie.

"Make that two," answered Bone. "Indian?"

"Yeah, Comanch…Got this one three times."

"I'd say mine's Apache and he's got two holes in him…Guess the girls were right, Renegades…Comanche, Apache and Kiowa."

"Well, this is two down," said Bodie as he walked over to Bone. "Wonder how many more?"

"Hard to tell…Suspect they were after our supplies."

"Most likely," replied Bodie. "Imagine they'll think twice before tryin' again."

"Wouldn't count on it."

"Comanch don't know when to quit…Why it took too long to get 'em on the reservation. Colonel Mackenzie had most of their horse herd killed off an' damn near starved the pore devils to death."

"Shame, I guess. They were just trying to protect their land they'd been on for centuries," said Bone.

"Yeah…Take their weapons an' leave 'em. We'll have the local law see to the bodies when we get to someplace we can contact 'em…Got a feelin' we ain't done with the redhides yet," replied Bodie as he stripped the Comanche of his guns, knives and ammo.

He and Bone headed back down to camp.

Six miles upstream below the cave where Bone, Loraine, Padrino, Milly and Bodie spent the night, the group of five nefarious brigands paused and listened to the gunfire in the distance.

"What the sam hill?" asked Rufus Pickens.

"Sounds like we may have competition," said Ace. "Comin' from the same direction these tracks is goin'."

"Unnh, rifle an' pistol fire," added Horse.

"Let's git a move on…Hate to miss out if'n they found anythin'." Ace bumped his horse into a lope through the melting sleet.

"Yeah, we want our pound of flesh…right, Bear?" Rufus asked his brother.

"Damn straight," replied Mayhab as he cracked his knuckles.

Bone's group had finished the sandwiches Loraine had made from the smoked ham Mary Lou packed for them along with a couple of loaves of sourdough bread.

They eased along the narrow trail that crossed the face of the cliff diagonally.

"Been a long time since any people besides Milly have been on this trail. As narrow as it is, I suspect just deer and goats have used it for years," commented Bone.

"Or mountain lions," added Bodie.

"Oh, yeah, forgot about them," said Loraine.

"Don't see any paw prints…Just deer and goat tracks like Bone said," agreed Padrino.

"That sleet would have taken out any tracks from bobcats or pumas…just saying," said Bone.

"I didn't see anythin' when I hid here before," added Milly.

"Well, I'm getting that same feeling I had when we found that statue…Like I've been here before." Padrino picked little Milly up and let her straddle his hip.

"Déjà vu all over again?" questioned a grinning Bone.

"Something like that." Padrino glanced at Milly's face and noticed a strange soft smile.

§§§

CHAPTER TWENTY-FOUR

BRAZOS CANYONS

John Horse led the five thugs along the muddy game trail that paralleled Rock Creek on its path down to the Brazos.

"Gunfire's stopped," said Gunn.

"Damn, little brother, glad you noticed. We weren't sure."

"Kiss my rusty, Ace."

Rufus and Mayhab exchanged glances.

The men spread out as they loped along the trail because of the mud being thrown back by the horses.

Horse slowed to a trot as the trail became steeper.

"What's the problem?" asked Ace from just behind him.

"Trail too steep and muddy, horses slip an' meby fall into creek."

"Oh…good thinkin'."

"Uhhh."

The group moved slowly along the tiny, almost nonexistent trail up to the small cave. Padrino had set Milly down as it was too dangerous to carry her on his hip.

The trail varied from fourteen inches to no more than five or six inches wide in places.

Milly glanced back at Padrino just behind her and noticed movement back down at their camp.

"Padrino, look," she exclaimed and pointed. "Injuns!"

He and the others stopped and looked back. Six Indians were approaching their camp.

"They waited till they saw us leave and moved down to raid our camp for the supplies and we're on the side of this cliff with no cover," commented Padrino as he drew his .45.

"An' no rifles," added Bodie who was in the lead.

"No choice, people...the best defense is a good offense," commented Bone.

"Thought it was the other way around, honey," stated Loraine.

"Do with what you got, baby...Least we have the high ground now...Let's give 'em hell." He opened fire with his 500 Smith & Wesson.

The tremendous roar from the .50 caliber weapon that accompanied the Indian in the lead to collapse to the ground, startled the other renegades.

"Lie down, Milly!" Padrino yelled as he and the others began firing rapidly.

Bodie, Bone, Loraine and Padrino, all crouched down as best they could with almost no footholds on the tiny ledge. Their fire on the hostiles was murderous and prompted a panicked return fire, peppering the side of the cliff around the five haphazardly.

One after another of the band of Indians fell to the fusillade from above.

Padrino shielded Milly with his body as he emptied magazine after magazine down at the renegades.

And then, the quiet was deafening as all the Indians at the edge of the camp were on the ground.

"Everybody hold," yelled Bone as he studied the six still forms below in the rapidly dispersing gunsmoke cloud from their rifles.

The sudden quiet was pierced by a shriek from Milly. Loraine worked her way back down to her and Padrino. The white-haired retired Marine was on top of the child. She looked up at Loraine, lifted her hand from Padrino's back—it was covered with blood.

"Are you hurt, Milly?" asked Loraine.

"No! No, not me!" she screamed. "It's my Padrino, my Padrino," came her heart rending response. "No, no...Please! Please, Padrino, wake up. Wake up, Padrino," Milly sobbed into his white hair just beneath her chin.

Five miles upstream, the five outlaws pulled rein at the sound of the gunfire again.

"Damnation, sounds like a war," shouted Ace.

"Group attacked," said Horse.

"Who in the hell?" questioned Gunn.

"Somebody else on the scout. Heard stories that they's renegade Injuns still down in these canyons," commented Rufus.

"Loraine, pull Milly out from under Padrino and then crawl over the top of me. I'm going to lie as flat as I can." Bone glanced back over his shoulder. "Bodie, get on up to the cave and help me when I get there with Padrino.

Loraine holstered her Kimber, reached forward to Milly's bloody hand, grabbed it and slowly pulled the waif partially out from under Padrino's limp body. She turned around on her hands and knees. "Honey, wrap your arms around my neck and hold on tight, can you do that?"

"Uh-huh," Milly said through her sobs as she worked her legs out from under Padrino's still form, rolled over, clambered on Loraine's back and wrapped her arms around her neck.

Bone was stretched out the best he could along the skinny trail allowing Loraine to crawl over his big body toward the entrance where Bodie had his hand sticking out of the opening.

He pulled Loraine and Milly inside where Loraine turned over and hugged the devastated child to her bosom.

Bone belly crawled on down to Padrino and knowing that he was too big to turn around on the tiny ledge, he grabbed the collar of his godfather's tough canvass Carhartt jacket, and then began working his way backward toward the cave opening, dragging the older man with him.

Inch by inch he moved, sweat dripping from his brow and falling from the tip of his nose, even in the chilly air. Bone's massive strength allowed him to not only maintain his purchase on the tiny trail, but to move along it backward, dragging a one hundred and sixty pound body. Padrino slid off the narrow ledge and hung there, held only by his coat collar in Bone's big hand.

He had done almost the same thing, but under enemy fire in Afghanistan, to pull one of his wounded squad members to safety. *Well, at least all the Indians are down and we're not gettin' shot at.*

Finally, he felt Bodie's hand grab hold of his moccasin covered ankle and help him as he wormed his way backward into the cave.

Loraine helped him to remove Padrino's jacket so they could get to the wound as a softly crying Milly lovingly caressed his face.

Loraine pulled her doeskin top up and ripped the bottom of her camo T shirt off, folded it and pressed it to the hole in Padrino's back just below his scapula.

She looked over at Bone. "There was foam in the blood."

"Damn." He carefully lifted the frail body up. "Go through?"

She nodded as she continued pressing the compress to the wound. "Must have caught a ricochet from the wall." Loraine folded up a second pad for the exit wound.

Bone opened his parfleche and took out another small leather pouch. He opened it and removed a vial of white powder. "Lift the pad up for a second."

Loraine lifted it while he sprinkled some of the powder on the entrance wound. He nodded at her to put the pad back down.

"Now the second."

"Powdered alum?" she asked.

"Yeah, got some from Marshal Lindsey after our wedding...Said he always carried some. Does essentially the same thing as the powdered kaolin clay and the treated gauze we used in combat, but actually, I think I like this better...Just keep pressure."

"What about the bubbles?"

He shook his head. "Clipped a lung...Can't do anything about that...needs surgery...and prayers."

Loraine put her face close to Padrino's nose. "There's almost no air coming out." She put her fingers on his carotid artery and watched the second hand of the watch she wore when they were slung back in time to 1898. Loraine finally looked up at Bone and Bodie and shook her head. "It's less than forty beats a minute and erratic."

"No, no, my Padrino," Milly kept muttering through her tears.

"Didn't the round I took in that stagecoach robbery hit my lung?" Loraine asked.

"Yeah."

"But, you saved my life with that energy transfer thing that Lucy taught us."

"And you used it on me when I caught some of the death ray beam from that killer in Gainesville a couple years ago."

"You only got a brush. The gold foil you put in your hat caught the most of it...I was a real Ned in the First Reader trying to use it."

Bone nodded. "But, Pard, you stopped my cranial hemorrhaging. That's what we have to do...His age is a big problem, but we got to try."

They made Padrino comfortable as they could and each started to lie down on either side.

"No," Milly interrupted with a firm command from behind them.

They glanced over at the young child and noticed there was something different. She had stopped crying. It seemed there was a slight glow to her golden eyes and she had the countenance of an adult.

She waved them away with a perfunctory motion and laid her tiny body on top of Padrino's chest and closed her eyes. In a few seconds a blue glow emanated from her body and then enveloped him.

The glow intensified to a point that Milly and Padrino were no longer visible inside it.

Bone, Loraine and Bodie were stunned as they looked at one another.

"That glow is ever bit as bright as when Lucy and Fiona brought Mason back from bein' dead," said Bodie.

"And you had already died too, when Lucy brought you back and it was like that," added Loraine.

"But, it's Milly...she's a child and a malnourished one at that," said Bone. "Where did she learn this?"

The bright blue glow continued for what seemed like long moments, and then finally, it slowly began to fade, and then vanished all together.

Milly was completely still as she continued laying on Padrino's chest.

Padrino took a deep breath, his eyes flickered, and then opened. He looked around in confusion and at Bone, and then down to Milly on his chest.

He put his hand to her face and wrapped his other arm around her frail body for a long moment, and then kissed her forehead. Padrino finally looked up at the others with tears in his eyes and rolling down his cheeks. His lower lip quivered.

Padrino's voice was a hoarse whisper and cracked as he said, "She's gone…Milly's gone…She gave her life for me…My Milly's…gone."

§§§

CHAPTER TWENTY-FIVE

BRAZOS CANYONS

"Maybe Loraine and I can replace some of the life force she gave you?" commented Bone.

Padrino looked down at the pale, drawn, almost withered body, shook his head and glanced up. "It's too late, Bone, she gave me everything she had." He held her to him. "There's not anything left, but an empty husk…There's nothing to work with…She's gone, Bone…I felt her soul leave," his voice broke as he finished.

"I'm so sorry, Padrino," said Bone as a lump grew in his throat.

He nodded. "Let's go down to the camp and get some rope to lower with. I want to properly wrap her in her own blanket. I want to bury her back at the ranch," said a wan Padrino as he stretched his back and wiped his eyes.

"You okay to make it down, Padrino?" asked Bone. "You look pretty rough…You lost a lot of blood."

"I lost my Milly, too," tears began to flow again. "I'll make it," he whispered as he covered her tiny body with his jacket.

Bodie led the way out and down the face of the cliff, followed by Loraine, then Padrino, and finally Bone. They all reached the bottom and headed over to the camp stepping over the bodies of the renegade Indians.

Ace and his crew rode around the bend forty yards upstream and reined up. Surprise registered on their faces.

"This must be the place, brother," said Gunn. "Didn't expect to come upon them so soon."

"Yeah, ya'll spread out," commented Ace.

The group of miscreants fanned out along the wide sandy beach that formed part of the flood area of the creek during high water times.

Bone leaned toward Loraine. "How are you on ammo, Pard?"

"One full mag plus two rounds."

"Bodie?"

"Full wheel and..." He felt along his belt in the cartridge loops. "Five spares."

"Padrino?"

"Four left in a mag."

"I got one speedload cylinder left and seven rounds in my belt...Let's see if we can talk our way out." He glanced at Padrino. "See if you can slip back behind us while I keep 'em talking, get some ammo...and grab a rifle."

Padrino nodded, faded behind Bone and walked into the camp.

"What can we do for you fellows?" asked Bone as the five men slowly walked their horses forward.

When they got to twenty yards, Bone spoke again, "That's far enough. I asked what we could do for you."

"Looks like ya'll had a bit of trouble," said Ace.

"Oh, we didn't...they did, though." He glanced at the six bodies.

"Renegades?" asked Ace.

"Most likely," replied Bone.

Bodie whispered, "The little gunhawk just removed his hammer thong."

"Noticed," Bone whispered back.

"Ya'll find somethin' up in that cave?" Ace nodded to the opening up the cliff.

"Not so's you could tell," replied Bone.

"Where'd the old man go?" asked Gunn.

"Oh, I think it was about his nap time," answered Loraine. "Looks like your face hasn't healed up much."

Gunn blanched and shot a glance at his brother.

"She the one that worked you over, little brother?"

"Naw, naw...uh...she was jest there's all."

"Thought you said they left before all them toughs in the saloon jumped you?"

"Well..."

Loraine laughed. "That what he said?" She looked back at Gunn. "You want some more…little man?"

"Damn you, woman…"

His right hand moved toward the butt of his ivory-handled Colt on that side.

"Wouldn't do that, boy," came Padrino's voice along with the sound of a cartridge being levered into the chamber of a Winchester as he stepped around one of the big rocks at the camp and aimed at Gunn.

"Now, I'm going to break one of my rules and ask you turds one more time…What do you want?" said Bone.

"I want a piece of your ass, feller. You look almost big enough fer me to tangle with…knuckles an' skulls…no guns…just knuckles an' skulls," said Maydab. "Ya'll kilt four of my nephews…an' yer gonna pay."

"And just who might you be, big 'un?" asked Bone.

"Name's Maydab Pickens…Most jest calls me Bear…"

"I can believe it."

"Can I have him, Bone?" asked Loraine.

"Oh, no, honey, you get all the fun...Let me have this one."

Gunn turned a deeper shade of red as his brother glared at him and John Horse chuckled.

"Why don't you boys step down, give your horses a rest from trailin' us, an' we let Deputy Bone here an' Bear...get acquainted," said Bodie.

"You knew we were trackin' ya'll?" asked Ace.

Bodie grinned. "Sure...Knew it from day one...Wanted to see what ya'll wanted."

"We want that treasure, that's what," said Gunn with a sneer as he dismounted.

"What treasure?" asked Loraine.

"That treasure what goes with the statue ya'll found," answered Ace.

"Oh, right, you're working for those two grifters my wife and I spanked and sent on their way. Didn't have the guts to come back themselves, so they sent some hired help...some inept and sissy hired help," commented Bone with a big grin.

"Sissy!" Gunn shouted. "We'll show you, sissy, after this big sonofabitch here gits through with you."

Bone unbuckled his gunbelt and handed it to Loraine. "Well, let's get to it." He moved to an open area of sand between the two groups and stood with his arms folded across his chest and waited on Bear.

The big, bearded, three hundred and twenty pound man in faded blue bib overalls with once red long johns underneath, dismounted, to the obvious relief of his horse. He wasn't wearing a sidearm, but he removed his battered brown fedora, hung it on his saddle horn, and stepped toward Bone.

He doubled up his ham-sized fists and took a roundhouse swing at Bone's head. Bone slipped the punch and countered with a hard left hook to Bear's jaw.

The big man stepped back a half-step and nodded. "Huh, good one." He grinned, showing his tobacco-stained teeth with one front tooth and an incisor missing.

"Uh-oh," muttered Bone.

The two behemoths circled one another. Bear brought his fists up in front of him like John L. Sullivan, but Bone carried his down, like Muhammed Ali.

Bear swung again and caught Bone with a glancing blow across the side of his head.

"Damn, that would have hurt," said Bone as he threw a straight left jab from his shoulder to Bear's nose. Blood flew in all directions as the blow splattered his nose to the side. The man just shook his head again and grinned.

He swung his left and when Bone ducked, he countered with his right, connecting with Bone's cheek, knocking him back and to the ground where he sat up with a walleyed look, blinked a couple of times, and glanced over to Loraine. "Maybe I should have let you take him, honey."

He rolled to the side just as Bear kicked at him with a size sixteen lace-up brogan. Bone crabbed around and jumped to his feet.

"Remember what I showed you, Bone," shouted Loraine.

"Now you tell me," he replied as Bear bull-rushed him like a giant defensive tackle.

Bone ducked and rolled under the bigger man, taking him to the ground with a thud.

"That would have been a penalty, Bone," yelled Loraine, with a big smile.

"I know, babe, but this is no rules knuckles and skulls," he said swinging a right cross to Bear's face as he was getting up. More blood flew.

"Now, I'm gittin' mad," said Bear.

"Oh, damn," responded Bone.

He charged again. Bone feinted to the right, then stepped left, out of the direct line of his charge and swung a hard right to Bear's midsection as he went by. The air left the big man with a whoosh and he dropped to his knees where his hand closed on the sand, grabbing a handful.

He staggered to his feet and flung the river sand in Bone's face, blinding him.

Bone quickly moved back with his hands to his eyes while Bear stepped forward and swung a right to Bone's head and then a left haymaker to his ribs. Bone spun around and dropped to his knees as Bear kicked a massive foot to his stomach, flipping him over on his back.

Bear dove on him, pummeling his head with both fists until Bone brought his knee up, hard, between Bear's legs.

Bear wobbled back and dropped to his knees, with both hands to his mangled privates, his eyes were wide as saucers while he mouthed a silent, *Ow.*

Bone stepped up and swung his fists in a right, left combination as hard as he could to Bear's head, spun in a 360, and delivered a roundhouse kick with his right foot to Bear's left ear.

The big man's eyes rolled up in the back of his head as he toppled to the side like a giant felled tree and lay still—his hands still held his crotch.

Bone bent over, put both hands on his knees, took several deep breaths and shook his head. He straightened up and brushed the rest of the sand from his face and looked over at Bear. "Had enough?" he asked the inert form.

"Damn you," came a yell from Bear's brother, Rufus, thirty feet away as he raised his double-barreled ten gauge to his shoulder and aimed at Bone.

Bone turned as the blast of the shotgun went harmlessly into the air when Rufus' head exploded like a ripe watermelon being dropped from a three-story building. It created a huge pink mist and scattered fragments of skull and gray brain matter on Ace, Gunn and John Horse.

Bone looked back at Loraine as she stood in a modified Weaver stance next to Bodie, both hands still gripped his .50 caliber Smith & Wesson pointed where Rufus had been. She had a wry smile on her face.

Ace and Gunn were momentarily frozen as the sound of the simultaneous ear shattering explosions reverberated from the cliffs of the canyon. It didn't last long.

Both men dove to the ground, drew their sidearms and started firing.

Bodie and Padrino quickly responded while Bone charged over to Loraine and tackled her to the ground. She rolled over, handed him his 500 while she drew her Kimber and double tapped Gunn in the forehead.

It was impossible to tell who shot Ace—Bodie or Padrino or both—but he had three holes, two to his head and one in his body as the brothers died, side by side.

Bone looked up at the sound of galloping hooves and saw John Horse disappear around the bend back toward the way they had come.

"Looks like the tracker's not having any more of it," Bone commented.

The gentle midday breeze carried the cloud of gunsmoke down the creek channel.

"Well, guess that takes care of that," said Bodie as he holstered his .45.

"Speak for yourself, Bodie, I'm going to be sore for a month. Never been hit that hard in my life."

"Better take a look, Bone," said Padrino as he pointed to Bear slowly sitting up and shaking his head.

"If he's willing, I recommend we let him take his brother's body back home and call the vendetta off," said Bone. "Don't think I want to do this again."

"We can ask," replied Bodie. "Be right back." He walked over and squatted down beside the giant of a man.

Padrino walked over with Milly's blanket and a rope in his hands. "I'm going back up and take care of Milly, if ya'll don't mind?"

"We'll go with you, you still look a bit shaky," said Loraine.

He nodded and led the way over to the cliff and started up the tiny trail.

When Padrino reached the cave opening he ducked his head and went inside where the main area was much enlarged. Loraine and Bone followed him.

BONE'S GOLD

Padrino was standing, looking down at his tan canvas jacket crumpled on the cave floor, when they came in—Milly's body was gone.

§§§

EPILOGUE

BRAZOS CANYONS

"What in…" started Bone as he stared at the floor.

Loraine pulled her tac light and panned it about the area of the main chamber. "I don't understand."

Padrino stood for a long moment, his focus was on his crumpled jacket. Finally he said, "I think I do."

Bodie stooped and entered the front of the cave. "Bear had enough too, gonna take the deal..." He looked at the floor, and then around the cave. "Where's the body?"

Padrino also pulled his tac light from a side pocket of his BDUs and flashed it to the end of the cave. The back appeared as if it were closed off by a cave-in sometime far into the past. There was a small opening at the top of the pile of detritus. He stepped over for a closer look.

"We need to remove this rubble," said Padrino and panned on the blockage.

"Just as well get started, then. If you think it's important, Padrino," commented Bone.

"I have the same feeling and am gettin' the same visions as when we found the statue."

"Well, step back, you don't need to be lifting this stuff," added Bone.

"I'll keep some light on the subject." He moved to the side of the tunnel and shined his broad beam on the pile.

"How have you been keeping your batteries charged?" asked Loraine as she slipped on her doeskin gloves.

"I keep my tac light next to the *moldivite* crystal. Seems to work just fine," answered Padrino.

"Let's stack the rocks on both sides as we remove them. Be easier if we have to replace them like up at the little cave where we found the statue."

"Good idea, Bone," said Bodie as he slipped on his gloves, too, and grabbed a melon-sized stone.

An hour later, they had removed enough of the material so they had a hole big enough at the top for Loraine to wiggle through.

She pulled out her light back out, crawled the seven feet to the top of the pile and wormed her way through the hole into the chamber on the other side. Loraine flashed her beam around.

"What do you see, Pard?" asked Bone.

"Oh, my God."

"What?" said Padrino.

"Ya'll will have to come in to see this…I can't explain it to you," replied Loraine. "Never seen anything like it."

Bone crawled up to the top and started rolling stones down to Bodie, who moved them off to the side. In a few minutes he felt he had a hole big enough for him to make it through.

"Believe I can make it and if I can then ya'll won't have any problems...Padrino, come on up, I'll help you through."

The seventy year old clambered up to the top over the rubble. Bone reached out a big hand and helped him to the hole.

"Padrino's coming through, Pard."

"I got him," replied Loraine.

She assisted him through the crawl space and to the other side.

Bone and Bodie could hear him gasp. "Oh, my."

"Go ahead, Ranger, I'm right behind you."

Bodie crawled through and was immediately followed by Bone.

The four of them stood at the bottom of the pile of rocks inside the antechamber. Bone, Loraine and Padrino all shined their powerful LED lights around the room.

Padrino dropped to his knees as he viewed the contents of the room.

Along the north wall were ten *Paracas* mummies in various positions. Some were in the fetal position, some were sitting with their knees pulled up and their arms around their legs and some were seated with their hands at the sides of their faces. Two were on their backs with their knees pulled to their chests. All the well-preserved mummies were wrapped in *Paracas* garb or blankets.

Each mummy had various personal items around them, some gold effigies, urns decorated with rubies and emeralds, walking sticks carved from whale ribs and even hammered gold death masks. Several were blond or red-haired.

Padrino got to his feet, moved to the first mummy nearest the entrance and kneeled again.

The mummy was seated in a lotus position with a multicolored fabric robe about her. Her hands were turned palm up on top of her knees. She had long blond tresses and a gold plate with a ruby center hung by black onyx beads around her neck.

"*Pachamama* - Earth Mother," he said reverently, and then looked back to the others. "It's Milly. She led us here. This is the most sacred treasure of the *Paracas* people. Death was an important aspect of our life…My people worshiped the spirits and bodies of our ancestors and we considered them holy. They brought them all the way from Peru to here when they split from the tribe."

"You mean the remains of their ancestors *are* the treasure?" asked Bodie.

Padrino nodded. "Much the same as the Egyptians. *Pachamama* or her reincarnated form of Milly was the high priestess who came north with the sect that Bone and I are descended from. She wanted to make sure our treasure was protected for all time…She was the last to be added to the sacred tomb."

"So, Milly and the others have been here over two thousand years?" asked Bodie.

He nodded. "We have to reseal the cave and make sure it will never be found again," said Padrino. "I have to do it for her."

"I know we can put all the rubble back, but how can we make sure no one can ever find it again before this area is under Possum Kingdom Lake when it's completed in 1941…But, what about between then and now?" asked Loraine.

Padrino got back to his feet. "When I picked Star from Pap Clark's horses he had for sale and made arrangements for a pack horse and panniers, I asked him if he would pick up six sticks of dynamite with caps and a roll of long burning fuse and pack them in the panniers before he brought the horse over to Faye's."

"You mean we've been haulin' dynamite with us all this time?" inquired Bodie. "How did you know we'd need it?"

Padrino smiled and nodded. "I just knew, Bodie."

"I've been all through those panniers, Padrino, I didn't see any dynamite," said Bone.

"It's packed in the bottom of the sugar box. I figured since none of us use sugar in our coffee and wouldn't use much in cooking, it should be pretty safe there," Padrino explained.

"What if it had caught a stray bullet in a confrontation with the bad guys?" mentioned Bodie.

Padrino shrugged. "Ah…Didn't think about that. Wouldn't have been pretty…Guess we were lucky."

"Always better to be lucky than good, my daddy always said," commented Bone.

"Guess we leave everthing as we found it, then?" said Bodie.

"Pretty much the size of it," answered Padrino.

Several hours later, Bone and Bodie were on top of the cliff above the cave entrance.

Padrino and Loraine were also on top, but, behind the tree line, Bone and Bodie were in front.

"Awright, got these three sticks well under these boulders on this side," said Bodie. "Caps inserted."

"Nice crack in the limestone over here, I lowered my three down about eight feet. Let's unroll twenty-five feet or so of fuze each and twist it together. Should detonate at the same time," added Bone.

"I hate it when someone says 'should' when talkin' 'bout dynamite," muttered Bodie.

They unrolled the fuse and twisted it together in the direction of Padrino and Loraine who were holding the horses back several hundred feet behind the tree line. Bone nodded at Bodie to head back as he took the disposable bic lighter he always carried for emergencies, even though he didn't smoke.

"Fire in the hole!" he yelled, lit the fuse, turned and sprinted for the trees while it sputtered and raced toward the two different charges.

He only got fifty feet away when the cliff shook as the dynamite detonated sending dirt, chunks of limestone and debris skyward and collapsing the top of the cliff down, burying the face of the cave completely.

Bone covered his head with both hands as he ran while some of the smaller stones peppered down on and around him. "Damn!"

He made it to the others with only a couple of small knots on his head.

"Cut it kind of close there, didn't you, honey?" said Loraine.

"Wanted to see how fast I could run, babe."

"Wasn't fast enough," commented Padrino. "You were running too long in one spot."

"I forgot about my bruised ribs. Should have let Bodie do it."

"Huh…Should have rolled out more fuse," Bodie replied.

Everything in the woods between what was left of the cliff and the group had gotten quiet since the explosion. The birds, cicadas, fussing squirrels, and other normal forest noises had momentarily stopped.

Bone's *William Tell Overture* ring tone pierced the quiet.

"The girls," said Loraine.

"Jake's Mule Barn, head jackass here," Bone answered as he touched the speaker icon.

"What the hell are you doing, Bone?"

"Oh, hey, Cap'n…We're just blowing up half the countryside. What's shaking?"

"I'm out at ya'lls ranch with the girls and they said they hadn't heard from you for a few days."

"You on speaker?"

"Am now."

"Hey, Stella, Peach," Loraine, Padrino and Bodie all said at the same time.

"Ya'll havin' a *Charivari* or a brush arbor revival meetin'?" asked Peach.

"I think a revival meeting is probably closer to the truth," said Loraine.

"Did ya'll find what you were looking for?" asked St. John.

"You could say so," said Bone.

"Dammit, don't play games with me, Bone."

"Tell you when we get back, Cap'n…long story," commented Bone.

"So ya'll are comin' back?" asked Peach.

"That's still under discussion."

"Damn you, Bone," came St. John's yell over the speaker as the phone went dead.

§§§§§

PREVIEW
THE NEXT EXCITING STORY
IN THE
BONE & LORAINE SAGA

BONE'S ENIGMA

CHAPTER ONE

FLYNN RANCH
1899

Bone and Loraine strolled, hand-in-hand, along a game trail that bordered Black Creek. The year-round water way cut through Mason and Fiona Flynn's newly purchased section of land that bordered Mason's sister, Mary Lou and her husband Cletus Wilson's property in Cooke County, Texas.

The Wilsons had taken in *Annuna*, the diminutive *Anunnaki* alien who was stranded when her spacecraft crashed at Aurora, Texas, April 17, 1897. Fiona had named her *Lucy* so she could pose as an abandoned child. The *Anunnaki* look exactly like the denizens of Earth, but smaller or maybe it could be said we look exactly like them—only larger.

The shrill cry of a hunting Red Tailed Hawk pierced the morning quiet over the Flynn Ranch as he flew above the adjacent pasture on the other side of the creek looking for his breakfast of a field mouse or a small cottontail.

Detective Darrell Bone and Inspector Loraine Rodriguez had been accidentally transported back 120 years through an ancient Amerindian portal located next to the present day lake, Possum Kingdom, in Palo Pinto, County, Texas several months earlier in October, 1898. They had since realized that after being partners for four years from 2014 to 2018, they were actually in love. They were married in December, 1898 in Gainesville in the back yard of Faye Skeans Boarding House.

Bone glanced over at Loraine. "Baby, I may say stupid things, sometimes…I know I laugh when I'm not supposed to."

They stopped and watched the bass underneath the clear water of the creek cruising along just under the surface, looking for a wayward insect or a minnow for a moment, before he continued,

"I know I'm a little crazy and probably won't change…Love me or not. But, I guarantee that I love you and it's with a full heart…and you can carve that in stone."

The 5'3" Hispanic beauty turned, reached up, wrapped her arms about the 6'8" giant of man's neck and pulled him down to her face.

She kissed him with passion, which he returned with fervor, and then leaned back and looked up at his amber gold eyes with her limpid brown ones. "My sweet Bone, you don't think I know that? Do you remember what I said to you while I was sitting on your chest after I threw you over my head over in Jacksboro, showing you some Kung Fu moves?"

"Pretty much. Kind of hard to forget…You said, you didn't want to wonder, you wanted to know what I was thinking every minute of the day like you wanted me know what you were thinking…"

Loraine interrupted him, "I said I liked open books...I love you, you big lug...I love your honesty...I love that you can't ever hide anything from me...Does that answer your final question?"

He gave her his patented enigmatic grin. "Well, I just wanted to say it outloud."

She kissed him again. "And I love you for that, too. It doesn't matter to me if we stay here in this time frame or go back home to 2019...I'll love you wherever we are..." She looked past Bone toward the ranch road twenty-five yards from the creek. "Who's that?"

Bone turned to see a man slumped in his saddle. His horse was slowly plodding toward the big two story native rock house in the distance where Bone, Loraine and his godfather, Padrino were staying with Bone's great grand parents, Sheriff Mason Flynn and Deputy US Marshal Fiona Miller Flynn.

"Walt," Bone exclaimed. "He's hurt."

The two ran the short distance to the walking blue roan horse, slowing to a walk themselves so they wouldn't startle the animal.

Loraine grabbed the reins and stopped the horse. "Whoa, Blue, easy boy."

BONE'S ENIGMA

"He's been shot," said Bone as he eased the long lanky ex-Texas Ranger, presently the High Sheriff of Cooke County, Walt Durbin, out of the saddle and into his arms.

Bone gently laid him on the ground and pulled out a clean handkerchief from his parfleche.

"He's been shot in the chest. Doesn't look like it hit an artery or anything, but it's still in there," said Loraine as she took the hanky from Bone and pressed it to the wound under his shirt and vest.

Bone grabbed Walt's canteen from where it was looped over the saddle horn of the Texas style double-rigged saddle and held it to the Sheriff's lips. Walt took a little sip and looked up at the big man leaning over him.

"Fancy meetin' you here, Bone," he whispered. "Just...Just comin' to see you."

"Who shot you, Walt?" asked Loraine.

"Bush...Bushwhacker."

"Do you know who it was?" inquired Bone.

Walt nodded. "B...Bank robber...He's from the future..."

Bone and Loraine exchanged glances...

§§§

301

OTHER NOVELS FROM
TIMBER CREEK PRESS
www.timbercreekpress.net

MILITARY ACTION/TECHNO
BLACK EAGLE FORCE: Eye of the Storm (Book #1)
by Buck Stienke and Ken Farmer
BLACK EAGLE FORCE: Sacred Mountain (Book #2) by Buck Stienke and Ken Farmer
RETURN of the STARFIGHTER (Book #3)
by Buck Stienke and Ken Farmer
BLACK EAGLE FORCE: BLOOD IVORY (Book #4)
by Buck Stienke and Ken Farmer with Doran Ingrham
BLACK EAGLE FORCE: FOURTH REICH (Book #5) by Buck Stienke and Ken Farmer
AURORA: INVASION (Book #6 in the BEF) by Ken Farmer & Buck Stienke
BLACK EAGLE FORCE: ISIS (Book #7) by Buck Stienke and Ken Farmer
BLOOD BROTHERS - Doran Ingrham, Buck Stienke and Ken Farmer
DARK SECRET - Doran Ingrham
NICARAGUAN HELL - Doran Ingrham
BLACKSTAR BOMBER by T.C. Miller

BLACKSTAR BAY by T.C. Miller
BLACKSTAR MOUNTAIN by T.C. Miller

HISTORICAL FICTION WESTERN
THE NATIONS by Ken Farmer and Buck Stienke
HAUNTED FALLS by Ken Farmer and Buck Stienke
HELL HOLE by Ken Farmer
ACROSS the RED by Ken Farmer and Buck Stienke
BASS and the LADY by Ken Farmer and Buck Stienke
DEVIL'S CANYON by Buck Stienke
LADY LAW by Ken Farmer
BLUE WATER WOMAN by Ken Farmer
FLYNN by Ken Farmer
AURALI RED by Ken Farmer
COLDIRON by Ken Farmer
STEELDUST by Ken Farmer
BONE by Ken Farmer
BONE'S LAW by Ken Farmer
BONE & LORAINE by Ken Farmer
BONE'S GOLD by Ken Farmer
BONE'S PARADOX by BUCK STIENKE

SY/FY
LEGEND of AURORA by Ken Farmer & Buck Stienke

AURORA: INVASION (Book #6 in the BEF) by
Ken Farmer & Buck Stienke

HISTORICAL FICTION ROMANCE
THE TEMPLAR TRILOGY
MYSTERIOUS TEMPLAR by Adriana Girolami
THE CRIMSON AMULET by Adriana Girolami
TEMPLAR'S REDEMPTION by Adriana Girolami

Coming Soon

HISTORICAL FICTION WESTERN
NO TIME to DIE by Buck Stienke (sequel to
Devil's Canyon by Buck Stienke
BONE'S ENIGMA by Ken Farmer

HISTORICAL FICTION ROMANCE
DAUGHTER of HADES by Adriana Girolami
ZAMINDAR and the LADY by Adriana Girolami
MILITARY ACTION/TECHNO
BLACKSTAR ENIGMA by T.C. Miller

SY/FY
ANTAREAN DILEMMA by T.C. Miller

Thanks for reading *BONE'S GOLD*. If you enjoyed it, I would really appreciate a review on Amazon. My Author Page is:
www.amazon.com/Ken-Farmer/e/B0057OT3YI
Email - pagact@yahoo.com

Personally autographed books available at my web site:
Web page: www.KenFarmer-Author.net

TIMBER CREEK PRESS